SHORT-LIVED

MICHAEL PRITSOS

Cover illustration by Josh Rottkamp

Cover design by Zographos

Edited by Little Green Eyed Press

To order additional copies please contact:
Nyx Writing Syndicate
nyxsyndicate@gmail.com
ISBN: 978-0-615-99395-9

For Jenni

SMOKE

The flint made a subtle grating sound as it sparked the butane-soaked wick of Jay's lighter. He brought the flame up to the cigarette between his lips, allowing it to dance in front of the paper before he inhaled and drew the thick smoke into his lungs.

Jay hated waiting.

What made it worse was that he stood in the bitter cold of Seattle's sidewalks. Dark clouds shrouded the street in a dismal grey, threatening to spill their contents soon, and Jay suddenly wished he had worn his raincoat. He pulled his beanie down until it nearly brushed against his eyelashes and hugged his thick black jacket against himself. Taking another drag of the cigarette helped warm his insides for a few more moments while he watched the building across the street.

He did not have to be patient for long. A middle-aged man stepped out of the office and onto the sidewalk with a carefree stride. The stride, and the fact that there was literally no one else around for blocks, told Jay this was whom he was looking for. Inhaling a final drag, Jay threw the cigarette to the side of the street and stepped out with a smile to greet the gentleman.

*

Startled, William paused for a moment before returning the young stranger's smile with an air of confusion. Once he saw the pistol in the stranger's hand, though, his smile twisted with perplexity. He dug deep down into his trench coat pocket. His revolver was still there. His fingers fumbled at wrapping around the handle of his gun. William never imagined that the pistol would be needed in his hometown. He had only bought it for business drives that brought him south to Los Angeles and San Diego.

"Your wallet, sir," the stranger demanded politely. He still wore the smile. It was not one of malice. Neither a grin nor a smirk, but rather a gentle smile. That look spoke more volumes of the thief's youth than the attempt at a beard on his face.

The shot surprised William more than the thief. He had never taken his gun from his pocket. It was still there, its hammer having fallen, with one less round to account for. William felt a knot in his stomach rise into his throat. He didn't remember wrapping his finger around the trigger. Or pulling it tight.

Jay dropped his pistol and stumbled backwards; fumbling with his heavy jacket to get a glimpse of the damage he had just received. He clawed at the fabric where he found the hole and opened it just enough to shove his hand inside to feel for his wound. Jay barely noticed the hard surface on his back as he placed his fingers into the tear to find the warmth of sticky fluid flowing out of him.

It was a brick wall that he slumped against, and he was not aware of anything unusual happening to his legs until they had already buckled and he fell on his backside. The gentleman who had fired just stood there above him. William wore no expression to show what he felt. No remorse. No pride.

Jay said nothing.

Nothing was worth saying. He sat there, in the cold with a hand on his abdomen nursing a wound he never thought he would know.

*

William stood on the cold Seattle sidewalk. A light rain began to fall as he glanced from the mugger back to his own hand being washed by the dark sky. Moving to the mugger's side, William's brown eyes met the panicked young blue ones. The rain would never be strong enough to rid the growing feeling from William's heart.

Grabbing his arms, William helped move the thief to a shaded area beside the doorway of that brick building. He could at least shield the thief from the freezing rain. Squatting, eyes on the dying man, William grabbed his cell phone from his left pocket. His fingers froze in rigidity when he saw the crimson flow leaking from the mugger's back. Two rivulets of blood were flowing freely from the thief to join the rainwater at William's shoes. He forced his stubborn fingers to dial.

Jay could tell from the look in the gentleman's eyes he was going to die. He had not expected to be sheltered from the rain, so at least there was that. He thought of his life back in Phoenix and the friends he had made there. People that would never be considered true friends by anyone. He pondered on the time he had wasted and the schooling that he could have gone through, and yet, chose not to. An easier life appealed to him.

Until now.

Jay groped at his pocket for a moment and saw the gentleman's eyes grow wide. Despite the obvious fear on the man's face, though, he made no move to run or shoot Jay, again.

Jay pulled the pack from his pocket and sighed. The paper carton was soaked in blood. Useless. When he needed them most, he had managed to ruin that too. Jay's blood rendered each cigarette inside useless. He felt tired. He rested his head against the wall. Once his chin was up and his head was back, Jay felt an influx of phlegm. Coughing, he hawked up a glob and sent the red mass into the gutter. When it was gone, another built up in its place.

*

"9-1-1 Emergen—"

William closed the flip phone and dropped it into his coat pocket. He ran his hand through his thinning brown and grey hair. The sprinkle turned into a drizzle. Looking back at the desperate blue irises lined by a spider web of red, he fought back tears. William wondered where this situation placed him. Would he be branded a killer? He had a license to carry a concealed weapon so he supposed there would be no trouble with the law. The thief was so young, though. What would people say? William's wife always warned him about carrying that pistol around and now it would seem she was right. This kid would not have shot him.

A hacked up ball of red phlegm splattered at his feet.

7

William shoved the ugly thoughts from his mind. They weren't important. Reaching inside his pocket, he withdrew a pack of cigarettes. William gingerly squatted next to the thief and placed a cigarette in his mouth. Settling on his heels, he placed another between his lips. He winced. He had been out of matches since his last smoke break. He had squeezed in three cigarettes instead of his typical one. With his daughter looking at universities all over the country, and the costs of such places, smoking a pack a day was the least of William's worries. Looking down, William saw the thief held a lighter in front of him. With a flick of the flint, it lit.

*

The smoke tasted exquisite as it rushed down Jay's bloodied throat and filled his lungs. He didn't bother knocking off the ash. It didn't matter. He wouldn't last through the cigarette anyway. He only wanted to enjoy the soothing feeling of the smoke's cradling embrace. That, at least, meant something.

Jay looked at the man squatting next to him. His killer. The gentleman took a long drag of his cigarette and pushed the smoke out into Seattle's chilling air. Uneasiness set plainly in his features. He turned to Jay and attempted a wan smile.

Jay nodded back before turning forward to watch the rain wash the street. The calm of the cigarette enveloped his body wholly. Inhaling, he watched grey wisps rise and dance off the tip of the cigarette paper. Slowly, he blew the thick smoke from his lungs and watched the thicker swirls drown.

POISON

Jason ran a ragged cloth over the mirror in small concentrated circles. It had to be perfect. Pure. Once satisfied, he asked for the baggy of powder. Dumping a little pile on the glass, he took the razorblade from his pocket and cut the powder into fat lines.

Jason motioned for Samuel to come closer. Samuel balked for a moment, his eyes transfixed on the mirror before his younger brother.

A bane sat in the center of the glass. Samuel pulled a five-dollar bill from his pocket and rolled into a crude straw anyway. Jason inhaled his first line and sighed, pushing the mirror to Samuel. The nineteen-year-old youth glanced towards his notebook and noticed an error in his writing. With one free hand he reached over and tore the page out. Absently, he crumpled it up and dropped it on the floor. It was a bunch of bullshit. All of it. Bent over, he hesitated when he caught his reflection. Redness fenced Samuel's brown irises and the dark circles under his eyes outlined his failure. His cheeks were rough with nearly a week's worth of stubble, and his lips almost blended in to his pale complexion.

"Why do we do this over a mirror?" Samuel muttered to no one in particular.

"What?" Jason replied as he leaned back in the torn leather chair that served as the living room's sole décor in the one-bedroom apartment. "Everyone does it on a mirror."

"Never mind," Samuel said.

Placing the rolled five in his right nostril and pinching the other closed, Samuel bent over the mirror and closed his eyes to avoid his reflection as he inhaled deeply. He blinked more than twice, leaned back, and nearly fell on the stained carpet. The cocaine penetrated his mind in mere moments. He watched his brother take his second line. The crude straw moved deftly along the glass as a vacuum, powder in its path disappearing quickly. Samuel's shabby life turned to one of ignorant bliss as his heart increased its pace.

The phone rang - an obnoxious pulse ripping through the apartment - until Samuel finally reached it. "Hello?"

"Sam?" asked a hesitant female voice.

"Yes."

"It's Jennifer. I need to talk with you. Can we meet somewhere?"

"My car doesn't run anymore," Samuel answered. A sudden dip in his mood told him that the powder started to fade already. Or was it just the embarrassment of his car's functionality? *One line just isn't enough anymore,* Samuel resolved.

"How can you get to work then? You know what... I guess... I guess that isn't important right now. I'll come to you. My parents gave me the car for the weekend."

"I can give you a couple bucks for gas," Samuel said slowly.

"Don't worry about it. I want to see you alone, okay? I'll

be at that corner store next to your house in fifteen minutes."

"I'll be there." He hung up.

Jason leaned over the mirror but looked at his brother. "Who was that?" Before he could snort any more powder or harass Samuel further, red droplets spattered on the mirror's surface. Jason put his hand to his nose. "Shit. I guess I'm done for the day."

"That was Jennifer," Samuel said. "I'm gonna' go meet her at the gas station."

"The gas station?" Jason eyed his brother as he stuffed a tissue up his nose. It was already spreading with crimson. "What if you run into Todd?"

Samuel shrugged. "I suppose it has to happen sometime."

"What the hell?" Jason's eyebrows lifted slightly. "Think of somethin' to tell him now. Just in case."

Samuel chuckled. "Coke isn't supposed to make you paranoid, you know. I'll only be a few minutes, okay?"

"Yeah, fine. Go ahead and go," Jason said. He smiled. "You know you don't always have to tell me where you're going. I'm not Dad."

Samuel felt a pit in his stomach at the irony of that statement. Their father left their mother five years before. He dabbled in drugs himself. She eventually left to New York to live with her sister and her family. It was as if she had just waited for Samuel to graduate before finally making the decision. She invited Samuel and Jason to come with her, but in his stubbornness, the youth refused to leave Phoenix. His younger brother always followed in key. For that reason Samuel felt guilty almost every day, as he stared at the younger boy snorting the drug that he had brought into his life. Jason stopped going to school altogether and worked part-time, sweeping up cut hair. The youth figured that was not necessarily bad for a seventeen-year-old, but Jason had no ambition for going back to high school.

Samuel knew he should cry for what once was and what he had made Jason become, but he had done it all before and it never made anything better. *I'm just coming down,* he convinced himself and ducked into their shared room to find clothes better suited for seeing a girl. Even if she was one he had to strain to remember.

He knew she had first come to their apartment with his friend Jacob. He was fairly certain she was pretty, but her habit of judging him and his younger brother made his doubt it. "Weird girl," he muttered to himself as he pulled on a cleaner pair of jeans. Drug haze or not, he still didn't know why she came over at all. When she did, she'd walk around with the same beer for over an hour and just look at his posters of different hip-hop artists. "That snoop!" he said, a flash of recognition. Jennifer was the one he had caught reading one of his trashed poems. He had been angry, but hid it well, and she had given the paper to him without any words.

The last time she had been with him, he could not see clearly. It must have been three or four weeks ago, but he could not be sure. They had sex. That he had not forgotten. She had probably drank too much, but that was also something he could not recall. He did remember her blabbing on and on about a depth behind his bloodshot eyes. That eventually led to a kiss, the kiss to a tug, the tug to hasty disrobing, and the disrobing to heated sex. She had called a couple times since, in attempts to probe his mind, but his constant state of highness always irritated. Why he even bothered going to talk to her now, he didn't know.

Eventually, he found a gray hoodie that wasn't too wrinkled and threw it over his white t-shirt. He did nothing about the state of his jeans. There were two quarter-sized bloodstains on the upper right pant leg, but the sweatshirt covered one of them and he figured the other was hidden almost as well from the shadows. Satisfied, he walked out of the apartment into the dim light of evening.

Samuel's trek to the corner store was fairly quick; time always passed briskly with a cigarette in his mouth. Plopping down on the curb, Samuel sat and waited in utter silence. He glanced behind him and watched a line of four people waiting impatiently at the store window. Posted on the window above his head was a sign that read "Help Wanted." The only thing missing was an arrow pointing down. *Yeah, that's me,* he thought with indignation. Few cars came and went, each person looking at him with more of an air of indignation than the next.

Even with my stubble, I still don't look of "legal smoking age," Samuel thought with annoyance. *Shit, I forgot to shave.* How

13

could he forget? He had just tried to clean himself up a bit before seeing Jennifer, yet overlooked cleaning up his own face in the process. Samuel inhaled deeply. *Who cares?* She was just a girl and not the most beautiful one he had ever seen anyway.

"Samuel," a gruff voice said from behind.

Samuel cringed but remained staring ahead.

"How interesting finding you out and about. I was just about to pay your apartment a visit."

Samuel turned slowly, his arms tensed to block an incoming strike. His own arms were scrawny and thin compared to the sizable ones his opponent offered. Nevertheless, it was always best to be careful. "Oh, hey, Todd. You were? You didn't call or anything…"

"You don't answer my calls," Todd replied. "I want my money. You and your faggot brother better give me something today or I'll take something more valuable from your apartment. I'm not fucking around this time."

Samuel had to bite back a laugh. *We don't own anything valuable.* "I would assume you weren't."

"Was that a smart answer?" Todd leaned in until Samuel could smell the vodka sitting rank on his breath. "I don't like it when people get smart with me, kid."

"I didn't mean it like that, I just meant that last time…"

"Last time was a walk in the park compared to this time, Sammy," Todd answered with a grimy smile. It went along perfectly with his shaved head, a yellowing wife-beater that hadn't known white in only God knew how long, and dark

14

cargo shorts.

Samuel inadvertently reached up to the back of his head where a small knot still resided after four months. "I don't... I don't have enough."

"You and your brother owe me seven hundred dollars, kid. You'd damn well better have something."

"I got five bucks, that's it; I swear. My car doesn't work anymore, so I lost my job and shit. I'm trying to get a new one... maybe I'll work here. You could come in and steal alcohol whenever you want until my shit's paid off. I swear it. It's not Jason's problem to deal with either," he added. "It was all for me, so he really had nothing to do with it."

"I don't give a shit which one of you two faggots is snortin' it all. I want my fuckin' money, kid."

Samuel looked to Todd's bulging green eyes for a moment before finding the sidewalk again. "I can't, I can't give you anything right now, man. You have to understa—"

Todd yanked Samuel to his feet and drew his arm behind his back, applying pressure to his wrist until Samuel felt like every tendon in his shoulder would snap. He did not mutter a sound for a moment, preferring to bite down on his inner cheek rather than give Todd the satisfaction of hearing pain. It was just a moment, though. Samuel finally drew in a deep gasp of breath along with a disgruntled sigh that appeased his tormentor for the time being.

Todd released his hold of Samuel's arm. The youth utilized all his remaining strength to keep from collapsing. "If

15

you don't have my money tomorrow, I'll kill you and your fuckin' brother. I don't care how you get it, but get it. Seven hundred."

"Wait, wait." Samuel bent over and nearly vomited. He thought of Jason's face the last time he'd take a beating from their cocaine dealer in front of him. The image of Jason taking that beating instead, or a worse one, burrowed its way into Samuel's mind. The youth straightened up and looked at Todd once more. "Take my car. You can... you can take my car."

"Your car? You just told me it didn't even work, dumbass. Do you think I'm fuckin' stupid or something? I told you not to get smart with me, kid."

"It's a 2000, so I'm sure it doesn't need much. I think there's something wrong with the water pump or some shit."

"What, are you a mechanic now?" Todd asked with a grin.

"I admit I don't know what's entirely wrong with it, but I know it must be something cheap, because it's not old at all. If you think of it as an investment, I'm sure you can make five times that seven hundred back. And then I won't owe you anything else."

"Baby Einstein over here," Todd remarked to a passing customer. The woman glanced their way for less than a second, before quickening her pace, as if whatever she needed suddenly became urgent. "All right, all right, Sammy. I got a little mechanic faggot who owes me nearly half-a-G anyway. I'll run his ass over there tomorrow and he'll fix the car, and have it outta' there by the end of the day. You'd better fuckin' be there and give him those God-damn keys though, kid. I swear to God, if you're not…"

"I'll be there."

Just feet away from them, Jennifer pulled up in her mother's minivan. Todd took one look at the girl and decided it was time to put on a show. Samuel was cautious to avoid eye contact with her should Todd find out she was more than just some random girl, but he was hit anyway. Todd's fist smashed into his cheek with a shuddering blow that threw the youth completely from his feet. As he lay on his back, Samuel only stared at the cocaine dealer while he attempted a clumsy pass at Jennifer. Upon failure, he left.

"That's definitely not the type of thing that I wanted to see pulling up here," Jennifer said, as she squatted down to help Samuel to his feet.

"Well, I'm sorry you were so turned off, because I was completely enjoying myself," Samuel replied, rubbing the immediate swelling of his cheekbone. A little blood gathered in his mouth and he took care to not let her see when he spit it in the nearby trashcan.

Jennifer was more than he remembered.

A flowered sundress complimented the curves of her womanly body, and a light jacket shielded her from the subtle chill in the air. Her brown hair was tied back in a casual ponytail, and her bright face was flattered by gray eyes and thick pink lips.

Samuel felt awkward standing so close to someone so

above him. He sat down on the curb and stared at the asphalt.

"You wanted to talk about something?" Samuel asked.

"Well, I really came here more to tell you something."

"All right."

"I haven't had sex in a long time…" she started.

"Thanks a lot. Three weeks isn't even that long in my opinion."

"That was four weeks ago, and I was talking about prior to that. Sam listen, I… I know you're going through some rough times in your life right now. I mean… whatever happened just now. I'm pretty speechless, actually, but like. I do… well, no. I don't, but I can have some semblance of understanding."

Samuel shifted his gaze from her face down to the pattern of purple flowers on her dress. His eyes finally came to rest on the drone of light traffic moving back and forth in front of the gas station. "What's your point?"

"I hadn't had sex in a while, and so I… four weeks ago was… it was a mistake."

"Thanks, again. If you wanted to drill me, you could just hit me like that asshole did. To tell you the truth, that's actually a little better than this," Samuel replied with a glare.

"Will you just shut up for a second?" Jennifer took a deep breath and paused. Unable to find the words she searched for, she inhaled deeply, again. "Okay. It was a mistake, because I wasn't on birth control."

Samuel's heart dipped. Or, did it rise? Sometimes emotions were confusing for him, as they were usually drowned out or snorted away. But his buzz was definitely gone. He had to say something though, the silence was getting louder. "Uh-huh…"

"I've taken the test three times, Sam. I'm… I'm pregnant."

He exhaled slowly and kept his bloodshot eyes fixed on the traffic before him. "Pregnant," he repeated.

"Yes."

"And, you're sure that…"

"Positive."

"Well, I was going to ask if you were sure I—"

"I know what you were going to ask. I'm not a slut, Sam," Jennifer said curtly. Realizing the irony of her words, she sighed. "You're the only person I've slept with in over half a year."

"Well." He took a cigarette out of his pack and placed it between his lips. With a flick from the lighter and a long drag, smoke began to fill his lungs and temporarily ease the troubled thoughts wracking his mind. When Jennifer moved from her downwind position he looked at her curiously. Realization struck home.

"You're not… I mean, you're k-keeping…"

"Yes," Jennifer said. She placed a hand on his trembling shoulder. "I know, Sam. I know it must be really hard; seriously, trust me, I know. I just, I have… morals."

"But, you're not even out of high school."

"I will be in five months, and with the clothes I'll start

wearing, people will only begin to notice by that time, anyway. Besides, why should I give a fuck what other people think?"

She's obviously given this some thought. Samuel chuckled at himself for his own stupidity. *Of course she's given it some thought; it's a baby.* "Do you... do you want me to be like, a part of the kid's life?"

"That's up to you. I wasn't about to force anything. I just thought you should know."

"I think I'd... I think I'd want to be in the kid's life."

"Then don't call it 'the kid.' It will be your baby just as much as it is mine, so long as... Well, I can't have you around, if you're going to be... you know. You need to like, figure some shit out. I mean, I know you have several months to do that, but soon would be nice."

"All right," he replied. As he said it, he knew he meant it. Samuel was still unsure as to his own self, though. He almost immediately regretted the two words, despite the fact that no promises were made.

"Just show me, okay? Don't just say it."

"Naw... I mean, yeah. I'll... I'll show you." Samuel straightened his back and went to clumsily shake her delicate hand. Jennifer pulled him in and hugged him then. His cheeks flushed light pink. This girl he hardly knew, someone who he had gotten pregnant just over a month after first meeting, pulled him in for a hug. He smelled the sweetness of her hair, and knew that she must have smelled the grubbiness of his, but he appreciated the embrace, anyway. "Will I see you again soon?"

"I should hope so," she answered with a soft smile. "I have to go. I haven't told my parents just yet, and I think I want to do this all in one swoop. They'll be pissed, for sure; but, I'm positive they'll support my decision."

"What would they think of me?" Samuel asked, with a cringe.

"I wasn't planning on telling them much about who the father is. Not yet, anyway," Jennifer said. He nodded silently. She patted his shoulder, and when he looked into her face she was smiling. "Call me soon, yeah?"

"Definitely," he said.

Jennifer's mother's minivan started quickly and sped off to join the rest of the droning traffic. Samuel stood lost for a moment. He walked inside the corner store, briefly, before going back to the apartment. He found his brother flipping aimlessly through the static channels they received. Without saying a word, he went into the bathroom and smashed the loose mirror into a hundred fragments of glass and feigned mercury all over the tiled floor, then walked into the apartment's tiny kitchen and began filling out a cashier's application.

Money

Zach ran his fingers through his thick, curly black hair. Circles under his brown eyes made his men uneasy. They stood awaiting instructions in his cousin's pool hall, their place of preference for discussions. He closed his eyes and thoughts to them, preferring the company of his eyelids to that of thugs and drug-addicts.

"Boss?"

He flung his eyes open and glared in Travis' direction.

"With Stanson dead, we should probably start—"

"We need to move before James and his crew do," Zach announced.

"That's not exactly what I was gonna' say, Boss," Travis said. Another shot from Zach's tired eyes and he knew to keep his mouth shut.

"They will move in on our territory now, we all know this. Jay Stanson's relationship with James was our last tie. That could've kept the peace between us. For a while, anyway. With him gone, there's no way of knowing when that son-of-a-bitch will start moving in on us and grabbing our clients. Travis, you'll handle the first assignment."

The lanky man stood up to his menacing five feet, eight inches. "What do you need, Boss?"

"East Phoenix is now open for business," Zach said with a forced smile. "I need you to do whatever it takes. Street corners, kickbacks, parties, whatever. Find someone who wants blow, and put it in their nose. You can even do a bit of sampling, if they already get their shit from James' people. Take one of these other two with you, in case shit goes awry," Zach said, pointing to the two young thugs in the room. *At least they look the part,* he thought with agitation. Swiveling in his chair, Zach faced another one of his guys sucking down cigarette smoke as if it was his life's source. "Jacob, all I need you to do is get a couple more people to have a constant flow of coke coming from us to them. Those York brothers should do as your first two customers, and other than that, you can pick your own people."

Jacob finished his cigarette and scrunched it down in the ashtray on Zach's desk. "The York's won't go for it anymore. They say they're done with that shit. The oldest one has some problems he's dealing with or some shit and the youngest one's in the hospital."

"Oh yeah, that's right. Well, good for them, I'm sure they'll make a couple of model citizens. I guess we don't have to figure out how we can swing them to our side anymore. Find others."

Jacob nodded and lit another cigarette as Zach turned to a third man in the clouded room.

"You need to come with me tonight. We're going to Mesa for a couple of business arrangements."

"Mesa is notorious for shitty coke," the young man protested.

23

"We're... expanding our horizons," Zach explained, with a casual wave of his hands. "Everyone can go now, except for you, Frank. I need to speak with you alone."

The portly man standing aside from the others stayed where he was, visibly nervous for no apparent reason at all. Upon first meeting him, Zach was almost certain that he was a cop and had even held him at gunpoint and searched him for wires or any weapons, but the pudgy man had nothing. Six months later, he was still loyal. Loyal, but nervous. *Maybe he's just a sweaty anxious bastard,* Zach concluded as he watched Frank await everyone's departure. *Plus, there's the fat thing.*

"Frank, I don't need you leaving our side of the city. You don't really look the part to be slingin' your weed on the Eastside. What I do need from you, however, is to go tell your buddy Steve I have another job for him."

"C-can do," Frank replied.

With a shift of his weight, the pudgy man waddled towards the door leaving Zach with a moment of silence. If only it had lasted longer. José came back in as soon as Frank left, letting the thick metal door slam shut behind him. He paused for a moment in the middle of the room, as if that would have been able to softly close the already shut door.

"When do we leave?"

"I suppose now is good enough," Zach said. He ran his fingers through his dark, curly hair and stood up from his chair.

"Are we stayin' there long?"

"God, hopefully we'll be there for less than two hours."

"I'll go warm up the car," José said before leaving. He closed the door excruciatingly slowly on his way out.

The chilled air bit deep and José wished that he had brought a thicker jacket, but he figured since they were going to Mesa, it would not be that big of a deal once he got back out of the car, anyway. He started Zach's BMW with a casual grace he had learned after being cuffed on the ear several times. Zach said he was always "jumping the gun" on their departures. He stared out at the sky while he waited. Winter was nearly there. Clouds gathered around the waning moon like a thick coat.

Zach strode out of the pool hall in his normal demeanor. The handle of a revolver was slightly visible, as his black jacket parted with a soft breeze. José said nothing as his boss climbed into the vehicle and inspected the fuel gauge. José brought the sleek car back from the shop exactly how Zach had ordered it to be. He made sure he was precise, now.

"I want no trouble with jakes, so don't go too far above the speed limit," Zach said as he strapped his seatbelt on.

"You got it," José replied, looking this way and that as if the cops would suddenly show.

Streets blurred into the freeway, and freeway blurred into the highway, and before José knew it they were close to Mesa. The streets there were a little more rundown and shoddy compared to those in Western Phoenix, and José knew that even those streets weren't exactly the best.

"Where to, Boss?" José asked. With a soft nudge, he pulled Zach out of the nap he was enjoying. Slowly his mind came back to the present.

"Are we there?"

"We're in Mesa. Now where do we go?"

"Southeast," Zach said and gave his driver the exact streets. "You can look at this map, if you want, but the streets are pretty basic."

José looked over the map and blinked away his drowsiness. They were close. It only took a few minutes to reach their destination.

"Is this the house?" José asked with a look of disgust.

"You're just full of fuckin' questions today, aren't you?" Zach mused. "Yes, this is the house. I'm sure of it. They're not exactly running an empire, but I think we can use their little enterprise for a mutual gain."

José looked at him strangely, but Zach did not care to explain and so walked to the front door. One backwards glance told José to take his handgun off safe. The house was quiet, and it took more than a couple minutes for someone to stagger to the door. The man who opened it was in his mid-thirties, and looked as if he had on the same wife beater and stained jeans that he would have been wearing last Thursday and the Thursday before.

"You Zach?" he asked. His teeth were a row of jagged yellow with brown spaces in between. All set in a pursed mouth that lay in the forest of a brown and white beard.

"Yes," Zach answered. "This is my friend, José."

"Ah, a homeboy!" the man shouted as he reached out to

26

shake José's hand. The Mexican driver did not look amused. He took the calloused paw briefly, anyway. "Well, c'mon in. We don't have any food right now, but I'm sure we'll have a bit for our bellies after tonight."

"If I find your company tasteful enough, I guess," Zach replied. The man either did not hear or chose to ignore it, as he gave the two young men a tour of his ragged home. Beer cans and cigarettes were strewn around the house, as if they were part of the décor. With the shoddy wallpaper and broken coffee-table, Zach would not have been surprised if the man actually thought the trash added to the home's flavor.

The last part of the tour involved heading downstairs, into the basement. Here was the real center of Zach's interest. Black tubes and wires were crisscrossed all over the floor and underneath dirty tables were beakers and test tubes neatly placed. Although they had water stains on them, Zach figured they must have been the things most recently washed in the house. *Thank God for that, at least,* he thought as he ran his fingers along the thick glass trays above extinguished burners and torches.

"Shall we talk numbers?" the rugged man asked.

"Shall we talk names first?" Zach replied.

"You can call me Billy, if you want," the man answered.

"Is that your actual name?" Zach wondered aloud with a casual chuckle.

"If you want to believe it is, then sure."

Suddenly Zach felt very out of place. He could not tell

what it was exactly, but he knew he at least felt foolish for giving his own name out to these lowlifes that had no intention of giving him theirs. It was all so impersonal and strange. He felt like a stream of police would suddenly rush into the house.

As if reading his mind, Billy said, "Don't worry man. Everything is legit, an' I've never been in any trouble. I just need to keep my own interests secure, you know?"

"I suppose I do," Zach answered. "Numbers, then?"

"Numbers, it is. I want twelve grand each time we exchange, which should probably be about once a month I'm guessin', and we'll even handle the shippin' for you."

"Twelve thousand is quite a bit, if you're thinking the amount of meth I am," Zach replied. "I'll do nine thousand?"

José took a deep breath. He knew his opinion was not wanted here, but he could hardly restrain himself. *Meth, now? I need a raise.*

"We're talking about ice, here, not some powdered bullshit," Billy replied.

"Ninety-five hundred."

"Eleven," Billy offered.

"Shipping doesn't cost you shit, and you know it. A civic can run back and forth from you to us for well under fifty bucks."

"It's risk."

"I'll do ten, but that's it," Zach said firmly.

"All right, all right," Billy grinned, and exposing his horrid yellow teeth. "Ten."

Zach shook his calloused hand and took one more look around. "What about a sample?"

"For yourself? You don't look like you'd be into—"

"Not for me," Zach replied heatedly. "For me to take back. Three hundred worth. I'll give you one-fifty."

"You're steep, for a scrawny little guy, you know that?" Billy said. He moved forward until his chest nearly touched Zach's.

Zach did not flinch. He stood unwavering and waited patiently. José started to slide his gun from his belt, when suddenly the big man laughed and clapped Zach on the shoulder. He moved over to a cupboard housing an inventory of processed methamphetamines. He took out a couple plastic bags filled with the notorious crystals and started to hand them over to the gangster.

"Wait…"

"I'm legit," Zach said irritably. *I'm not gonna' smoke that shit, but if he wants proof…* He took out a spliff of mixed weed and tobacco and sparked it up.

"I suppose no cop would be gettin' high no matter what drug they were tryin' to snag people for," Billy conceded. He gave the bags to Zach and received three fifties in return.

Zach took one more puff and put the spliff in a cluttered ashtray without even finishing a quarter of it. Better to always be on the alert. Even if he was peddling dope of any kind, that didn't mean he had to use. Billy smirked a farewell and took the joint back out of the ashtray before they left. He pulled the lighter from his pocket and sparked the cherry again.

José maintain his silence on the drive home, keeping his feelings about the entire thing to himself. The shipments would begin the following week, in accordance to Zach's instructions, and after that the cocaine they distributed on West Phoenix's streets would be child's play compared to this new addition. José couldn't help but shake his head. One of the cheapest and dirtiest drugs known to man, and they were buying it by the pound. *That's just the beginning, too,* José thought alongside a deep inhale. Zach was asleep at his side, his conscience unburdened by the distribution of filth.

His boss may have his own set of morals in terms of drug use but he never stopped to wonder if he was selling his soul. Or, maybe he just didn't care.

Would you do the same thing, José? he asked himself as he merged onto the highway. *Would you go the same route for money?* Quietly so as not to disturb his sleeping boss, he arched his back in the driver's seat and pulled the wallet from his back pocket. *Light, as usual,* José thought dismissively before he placed it into the cup holder. *I gotta' ask for that raise.*

LIFE

"You ever get tired of this shit, man?" Joey asked.

The twenty-two year old man, Steve, finished taping the leather grip of his wooden baseball bat and slid it into the back seat in total silence. He closed the back door of his trashy car and opened the front one. He turned back to his younger cousin, "A man has to learn how to protect his investments."

"Investments?" Joey looked incredulous. "What are you invested in?"

"Living," Steve answered shortly before getting in the car and turning the ignition. It jumped to life, but not without a few coughs. Joey shook his head and gave a casual wave as he watched Steve take off.

It was a bit of a drive, but nothing that the quarter-tank of gas could not handle. Dimly lit by a setting sun, the funeral home looked twice as ominous. Steve's dark eyes darted back and forth along the front of his car, as if searching for the dead rising from their graves. He pulled his cap down farther so his eyes were more shaded under the bill and parked in a spot barely visible to those weeping on the grass.

"You're late," a chubby young man informed him before he fully stepped out of the car.

"Stanson was never a friend of mine anyway, Frank," Steve replied. Pulling out a cigarette, he lit the end and took a long drag. "What's the news?"

"Jay was shot trying to mug a guy up in Seattle," Frank said with a shrug. "They flew his body back to A-Z for the burial."

"I'm pretty sure I'm clear on that. I'm talking about this other asshole. The dealer. Todd, right?"

"He's not here," Frank answered. "He's afraid that one of our boys'll jump him since he put one of the York brothers in the hospital."

"Who?" Steve asked.

"The York brothers. Sam and Jason. They live in Phoenix and were apparently buying most of their blow from him. After some bullshit upset, he put the youngest one in the hospital. It wasn't even over money; it was supposed to be some fuckin' warning or some shit even though they didn't owe him anything anymore. Zach says both of them are clean now, though. Todd has had his hands in other shit, as well. He's one of James' top earners."

"Well I guess this information is all pretty worthless, since he's not here," Steve replied.

Frank looked back to the funeral where Jay Stanson's mother sobbed and berated herself with a string of profanities over her failure. Sighing, he turned back to Steve, "I wouldn't necessarily say that. You should probably know who your target is inside and out; am I right?"

"That's actually the stupidest thing you've ever said, Frank; and trust me you've come up with some fuckin' doozies. The worst thing for someone who plans on killing someone else to do is learn as much about that person as possible. What if I start to like the guy?"

"He's a killer."

"So am I."

"Never mind, then. I guess that was a bad example. How do you do what you do, anyway?" Frank inquired.

Steve sighed. "I'm good at what I do, and I feel like I have been put on this world for a purpose. With one swing of my bat, I can put a grown man out of commission, forever." His voice was monotone. He had explained this more than once.

"But, why?"

"Why is the sky blue, Frank?" Steve asked with a shrug. "Why is grass green? What is the meaning of life? If life itself is a question, then I bring the answer to everyone's question. I just only give the answer to a few."

Frank smirked with disbelief. "How can you answer everyone's questions?"

"No, you moron; if life itself were a question, then the answer to everyone's question would be the exact same." Steve paused for a moment, waiting for the statement to register in his pudgy friend's mind. "Death, Frank, death. Death is the answer to life. Everyone receives it. Some get it quicker than others."

"I guess I just don't think it's your place to bring death to someone, Steve. God should be the only one who can do that," Frank declared.

"Then what the fuck are we doin' here?" Steve asked heatedly. He swiveled abruptly to leave.

"Wait."

Steve sighed. "Are you and I so different? I could ask you if you got permission from God to sell pot and speed to little kids on the corners, because I'm guessing you don't have that right. You do it anyway, though, and make money."

"W-well I h-have to," Frank replied. "Zach doesn't ask that much of me, he just wants a little bit of drug-selling from my angle and feeding others information. I just, I just do what I'm told, man."

"Are we so different?" Steve asked once more. He took another drag of his cigarette and tasted the butt. He flicked it away.

"The funeral's ending," Frank announced. "Don't you want to pay your respects to Jay's family?"

"Go ask if they got his gun back," Steve said. "I could use a nice gun."

Frank ignored the jest and ran up the minute hill to converse briefly with Jay's mother and little sister. For a short time, Steve watched his portly friend trying to give condolences for what had happened to the thief; but eventually he grew bored and decided to watch the traffic instead. There was probably no fix on where Todd lived yet, and so it would be pointless to try and prepare for an assault. The only reason Steve figured he could get away with it earlier was because most people showed more respect for the dead than to kill someone else at the funeral home. Steve smiled. *I'm not most people.*

Frank's tenor voice snapped him out of his delusions. "You ready?"

"What?" Steve looked at his friend strangely. "Where's your car?"

"It's at the shop, so I figured you'd be able to take me to Zach's. It's only a couple of miles."

"I'm pretty low on gas…"

"I'll give you a couple extra bucks," Frank replied. "Let's go grab a burger real quick, though."

"I literally have no money," Steve lied.

"I'll grab you something, you fuckin' bum," Frank said with a laugh.

"Says the man who needs a ride."

"Let's go, let's go," the pudgy man climbed into the passenger seat and instantly began fiddling with the radio.

They pulled out of the funeral home and started down the street at a steady speed. Nevertheless, the pair hit every single stoplight along the way to a burger joint. Steve sighed agitation. To top off the traffic, Frank kept playing with the dials on the radio. Darkness swept over Phoenix, and the only thing keeping the city illuminated were the streetlights and office buildings still lit up with their employees' dedication.

"Will you find a fuckin' station?" Steve asked. A rock solo started blaring through his factory speakers. "Leave that. I like this song."

"This song is fuckin' gay," Frank noted as he changed the station again. "What have you got in your player?"

"A mix of love songs," Steve answered facetiously.

"Homo," Frank replied, oblivious. His chubby fingers hit the dials once more, "Now this is... Look out!"

Steve slammed on the brakes to avoid smashing into the vehicle in front of him. Behind his car a van came to a progressive stop that just kissed his rear bumper. The driver of the first vehicle in line was burly, and when he stepped out of his car instantly slid a tire iron into view. The passenger strode out simultaneously with his right hand wrapped in a heavy chain. Steve's stomach somersaulted when he glanced back to the van behind them. Two men were stepping out of that vehicle, as well.

"Shit," Steve said abruptly. "Glove box. The glove box, Frank; fuckin' open up the glove box!"

Frank did as he was told and popped open the glove compartment. Inside were two butterfly knives and a set of brass knuckles. The driver-side window smashed. Shards of glass went flying into the car as Steve reached in the backseat for his bat. He slid it out and with a morbid crunch opened up the nasal passages of the man who had broken the window. As the attacker charged forward to hit the driver, the door flung open and sent him flying to the ground. The bat swung twice.

Frank looked around, while his companion used all his strength to bludgeon a man's skull into the ground. After sliding the brass knuckles over his chubby fingers, Frank gripped a blade in each hand and decided to step out and take whatever blows were to be had. The men were not moving towards him, however. They padded their way to Steve and drew their own crude weapons, leaving the portly young man standing dumbfounded beside the car.

I could run now. Maybe they won't even kill him, Frank thought. *No, you fool. You heard the sound of that man's head as the bat came down the second time. There's no way they'll let him survive. I have to fight back. I have to.* His legs moved forward uneasily as if they were made of gelatin. Frank thought he would fall flat on his face, until he saw that the three enemies had gathered around Steve. They were now just waiting for him to strike at them, before they would each take turns beating him to death.

"Look, the fat-fuck has the balls to come and face us," one of the men said on the other side of the circle.

Frank searched his surroundings. Bystanders were either turning to run or already doing so, although a few of the more shocked ones were standing in horror to watch how the scene would turn out. *Cell phones you morons. You must have cell phones. Call for someone!* He wanted to scream at them. Frank tightened his grip on the knives in his hands and felt his fingers strain white against the walls of each hole in the brass knuckles.

"Run, Frank," Steve said as he scanned his surroundings for any movements from all angles. "Just run."

Frank shook his head no and flung his hand forward in a failed attempt to stab one of the closer men with the blade. Instead of punching through flesh, he felt his hand twisted back, while a chained fist slammed into his temple and sent him into darkness. Another crack resounded as Steve's bat hit his attacker, but that was it. All was still and quiet for a moment before Frank heard more cracks and grunts. Frank's heart leapt for joy. *Steve did it! He broke through,* he thought until the blows were brought down on him as well. He tried to scream for Steve to stop, that it was him he was hitting, when he realized that Steve was not holding the weapon. His voice caught in his throat and the strikes kept raining down.

The darkness was all encompassing. It took Frank and shrouded him, even protected him from the pain of the remaining strikes he knew still pounded into his soft flesh. The bludgeons to his head were something of a relief, pushing him into a feeling of floating. It felt like hours he was at the hands of those men, but Frank knew that made no sense. Another pound came down on his head, darkness scattering with a glimpse of faded light. The darkness began to envelop him once more until suddenly light flashed everywhere. He reached out to embrace it as all sound died around him.

NIGHTLIFE

The truck made a soft sputter within the hood as it came to a gradual stop just before a two-story house. The residence had no lights on outside to illuminate the night, or give away a warm presence of people; but the gathering of vehicles perched along its driveway revealed more than enough. This was the place. As the key turned left and the engine spat and ceased, the sounds from inside the house filled the noiseless atmosphere in the truck.

"You're sure about this?" Gino asked. The small Italian man sat in the passenger seat with a distrustful look on his dark face as he stared at the house.

"No one's gonna' do shit," Travis replied as he stepped out of the truck. The doors to the old Ford banged closed before both men walked to the house's oaken front doors.

The smell of beer and cigarettes permeated the atmosphere inside the two-story home as the pair cautiously walked inside. They were greeted well enough by a couple people who slightly recognized them. But even still, Travis noticed that Gino kept his hand firmly in his right pocket, where he usually stowed his knife. Dim lighting cast shadows all over the room from where people stood in front of the light fixtures. Travis' eyes darted back and forth in search for familiar faces.

Rap music played throughout the house accentuated with

a heavy bass that nearly shook the foundation. Travis knew he had heard the artist before, but he could not remember who it was for sure. He nodded to Gino and they both trudged over to where the beer was being distributed from a large keg - kept cool in a kiddie pool - swimming in more water than ice. Each one of them took a cup, in turn, and had their sips before spotting where they would make their destination for the night.

"Excuse me, bro," Travis said as he placed his hand on another young man's shoulder. He gave a brief nod of acknowledgment and stepped aside to let the two outsiders pass him by.

Three young girls sat around the coffee-table with cigarettes in their right hands and beers in their lefts. They had that prissy look about them that displayed a life of privilege. With short skirts and spaghetti straps in spite of the weather, Travis knew he had made the right choice. He made his way over to them with a casual grin on his face that hinted at a slight interest in their personalities, as opposed to everything below their necklines. Two of the girls gave polite smiles back, but the third one gave a devilish smile of her own to compliment his. *Too bad she's not the best looking,* Travis thought. *Oh well, that's not what I'm here for, anyway.*

"Have you guys ever been happy?" Travis asked as he sat down opposite one of the girls. He was short compared to most guys, but his face looked like that which you would find in a Greek statue and his physique was not far from the perfection achieved in those marble sculptures, either. Gino took his place behind his friend's chair, keeping a wary eye on the door and the rest of the party in silence.

"Have we ever been happy?" one girl asked. "What kind of question is that?"

"I mean truly happy," Travis answered. Saying the line as if it had been used time and again, he continued, "I have something that can make you truly happy."

"If this is some kind of stupid line and you end it saying your cock can make us truly happy, I'm really not impressed. And, I also really doubt it," the same girl replied. Her friends chuckled.

Travis hid his agitation well. "What's your name?"

"Stephanie," the girl replied. "These are my friends Kayla and Amber."

No point in beating around the bush, he thought. "Have you ever done blow?"

Stephanie looked to both of her friends and then back at Travis with a nervous eye. He looked her up and down. She was a cute blonde girl, and fairly skinny. *In this day and age, that doesn't tell you shit, though. Better stay away from judging books by their covers,* Travis resolved. He watched as her gazed flickered from him to the floor and back again. He imagined his pencil lightly tracing the circles under her eyes, transforming her from the made-up party girl she tried to be into her own reality on a sketchpad. It was apparent that Stephanie was hesitant. The brunette introduced as Amber visibly attempted to look away into the crowd, pretending she had never had anything to do with the conversation. The other blonde, Kayla, seemed to still be entranced by Travis' appearance. She gave him a second fleeting smile, hoping he would chase her down with another of his own.

"I have," Stephanie finally admitted.

"Do you want to do it, again?" Travis asked. Quickly he turned to Kayla before Stephanie could respond with a no. He had to secure his seat with these girls. "What song is this? I feel like I've heard it before."

"The rapper is Big L," the girl answered. "The song's called 'Street Struck.'"

"Ah," he replied, remembering. "East Coast rap." Turning to the interrupted Stephanie he asked, "So, do you want to or not?"

"I don't, ah; it's hard to explain," Stephanie answered.

"You're tied into some other fuck, no doubt," Travis assumed.

"Yeah, I only get my snow from one guy," she admitted.

"Well, let me tell you a secret," Travis said with a smile as he leaned in. "What I have is much better than anything you're going to get on this side of town. It's cleaner, too. The high will last longer. It hits you harder too. I'm just saying... Why would you want to be tied down to some dumbass, just because he sells on this side of Phoenix?"

"I just... people don't really go against him," Stephanie replied. Anxiety hung on to every word she said, and Travis took that as his cue to bring out his bag.

Gino scanned the party without a bit of anxiety etching his olive toned features. He appeared casual, used to this kind of lifestyle, and Travis supposed that in a sense he was. Only subtleties in the twitch of his eyes gave his close friend the indication that he was uncomfortable. It wasn't every day they were on the wrong side of town trying to take business away from some competitors.

White powder lay inside Travis' bag like a heap of addicting flour, and he dumped a little mound smaller than an ant pile on the coffee-table. A couple guys sipping beer looked over at the table and then went back to their conversation. Travis began cutting up the cocaine with a razorblade he always kept in his wallet. Stephanie beat him to it when it came to getting out a bill. She rolled her twenty quickly and with an easy nonchalance, placed it in her nose to sniff her first line.

Stephanie blinked her eyes more than once, as she let the cocaine sink in. Travis sat and watched before offering for Kayla to do some, as well. Kayla leaned in and snorted a line before slumping down against the back of the couch.

Hook and sinker, Travis thought with a grin. He dumped a bit more of the cocaine down on the table, and after cutting it into two equal lines of white, he silently watched the two young women indulge once more. The brunette, Amber, sat nearly with her back to them as she sent text messages and played with her hair, occasionally taking a sip of beer or a drag from Stephanie's cigarette.

"We should go soon," Gino whispered into Travis' ear.

His friend nodded briefly in response.

"How about it, ladies? What do you think of what I have to offer?" Travis asked. The question, coupled with the high and the dealer's sly smile, gave the girls no alternative.

Kayla smiled and ran her hands through her blonde hair. "It's good. Very good, I mean."

"Definitely better than anything Todd has given us," Stephanie admitted.

"You want to take my number then, and drop that asshole?" Travis asked.

"He's gotten violent with a couple of his people before, though," Stephanie said with a newfound tone of worry. "Even girls we know say that he's gotten rough with them. What would we tell him?"

"Tell him you're quitting," the dealer answered with a shrug. "If you guys need protection, I'm sure I can handle that for you, as well. All you have to do is just buy from me."

"How much for these four lines?" Kayla inquired. She unrolled the powdery bill in her fingers delicately, as if it too could crumble into dust.

"First time's free," Travis replied. He slid a piece of paper with his number carefully written in black ink. No name.

Both girls thought their jaws would hit the coffee-table. This man was truly like no other dealer they had met before.

"Oh my God," Kayla said. "You are seriously, like, the coolest guy."

Travis laughed. "Thanks."

"Are you sure there's nothing we can do for you?" Stephanie asked. She wore a devilish grin and never noticed the death glare Amber gave her.

"No," Travis said reluctantly.

Gino started pulling him towards the door. "C'mon, we're done here."

"Without even finishing a beer, I made two new customers," Travis informed Gino once they were out of earshot from the girls. "From the way they wolfed down those lines, I'd say I made a couple fiend customers, actually. If word from them spreads, maybe I'll have three or four more added. That drops more off Todd's tally, as well."

"We can only hope," Gino said.

Travis dropped the remainder of his beer into the trashcan and began his walk outside. The crowd of teenagers and young college students parted as he made his way to the door. He was almost sad to be leaving. He had not actually participated in a young people's party in some time. It was usually in and out; and for some reason he always felt that the real fun would only begin when he was gone. He looked around at some of the teenagers in the crowd he walked through, singing along to the lyrics of another hip-hop song. Other youngsters were engaged in their own conversations. Two new partygoers arrived just as they were leaving; one being careful to plant his shoulder into Travis' as he walked through the door.

"Who the hell was that?" Travis asked as he rubbed the numbness from his shoulder.

"Patrick and Wes," Gino answered. "Friends of the dealer those girls were talking about."

"Todd?" Travis had to clarify.

"Yes," Gino replied.

Fear started to grip him for a moment but he let it ebb away into nothing. As they approached his truck, Travis noticed that his front left tire had been sliced and the air was almost completely drained. He gritted his teeth. "Mother fuckers."

Gino looked back to the house and drew the knife from his pocket.

Travis glanced at Gino's hand clutching the knife and scoffed. "Put that away for a minute, man. We need to figure out what we're doing here."

Gino snapped out of his trance and folded the blade back into the handle before stuffing it back into his jeans pocket. He kept staring at the house they had just left, watching for any movements, like the home itself was going to lurch out and attack him and his companion. The sun had set hours ago and other than a few lights inside and the occasional shadow passing in front of the window, there were no signs of life. Gino inhaled deeply as a shadow paused in front of the window. Travis' phone rang.

"Yeah?"

Gino kept his dark eyes on the house, only glancing briefly at his friend while he continued a conversation with someone on the other end. It sounded dramatic, and each response was quick and sharp, so the young Italian knew that something had gone wrong. The pair who slashed Travis' tire were somewhere inside that house, probably staring through the window and laughing at him and his friend standing idly next to a nearly useless vehicle.

Travis' voice snapped him back to reality again. "Gino."

"What?"

"That was Zach. Steve and Frank were murdered yesterday. He says no one knows for sure who did it. The attackers had put mud all over their license plates and left before any cops could get there," Travis explained. He sounded tired.

"Steve and Frank?" Gino could not believe it. "Dead?"

"Yeah," Travis said as he ran his hand through his dark hair. "Zach thinks Todd had people do it, since they were after him anyway."

"Or, just directly from James," Gino suggested. "Todd works for him and with Stanson dead up in Seattle…"

"That had nothing to do with us," Travis argued.

"What does that matter? James hates Zach. Always did. And Jay always kept the two of them amicable, at least. Now that's done… Frank and Steve dead, though. I can't believe it. Regardless, Patrick and Wes may have been the ones who did it," Gino concluded, looking again at the house where the pair were probably moving around drinking and exchanging stories. *Probably stories about killing two of my buddies.*

"May have? I'd put money on it. It's not just knifing tires

tonight," Travis said. He cracked his knuckles and moved to open his truck. Leaning inside for a moment he pushed aside a book of sketches and a handful of charcoals. Gino glanced at the discarded art for a moment while he played with the knife in his pocket. *He's good,* the short Italian thought with a smirk. The piece he saw looked rushed, but showed an exquisite detailing of an elderly couple sitting on a park bench. Travis found a red tank and stepped back onto the street again with an empty beer bottle.

Gino knew exactly what to do without any words being said. Tearing off a strip of cloth from the bottom of his shirt, Gino waited for just a moment as Travis poured gasoline into the bottle until it was near the top. The young Italian moved in and stuffed the cloth fully inside to get it soaked well in the fuel, and they did not have to walk far to find Wes' car. It was an older sports car and a convertible, though Gino could not tell really much else about it. *Doesn't matter, this car won't be on the road anymore after tonight,* he thought with a grin. Flipping his lighter open he lit the rag and let the flame pick up momentum along the cloth. One well-aimed brick smashed through the driver side window to expose an opening for the Molotov cocktail.

Gino chucked the bottle swiftly and it smashed to pieces against the inside of the passenger door, erupting in a small burst of flames that stretched along the vehicle's interior and already started licking the cloth roof with orange tongues. It only took seconds for the blaze to start pouring out of either side, and Gino watched just yards away with a silent awe as it tore apart the insides of their enemy's car. A bang from under the hood threw him off balance and rendered him deaf for a moment. Despite the immediate shock he felt, there were no burns on his body. Travis' hand lifted him to his feet and they both began the trek back to the truck.

"How can we leave with your tire like that?" Gino asked.

"It can still drive, but we're not gonna' leave just yet," Travis replied as he reached into his truck once more for a set of brass knuckles.

"That's what I like to hear," Gino said with another grin.

*

The second explosion was just that of a tire being popped. Oddly enough, it was not until after that one had sounded that the two men rushed out of the house. Wes shouted in fury and immediately pumped his legs toward the two men standing next to the old truck. Gino leapt forth first, meeting Wes with a flurry of punches that connected well with his jaw and stomach and sent him back for more than a moment. Wes circled the small Italian for what felt like an eternity, taking his time to wipe off the blood that accumulated in the corner of his mouth.

The click of a hammer sounded then in the dark of the night. Wes turned to find Patrick leveling a revolver at one of their opposition's chest. Travis had not even gotten a shot in with those brass knuckles strapped to his hand before he was stopped with the threat of death. He raised his hands in the air, all the while saying nothing.

The Italian, Gino, rummaged through his pocket, but Patrick kept his attention on Travis, and never even thought to move the gun. *What is he doing?* Wes wondered. He started to turn to the gunman at his side when a flash of silver went by his head and landed in his companion's shoulder. Patrick stumbled for a moment and grabbed at the blade in his arm before finally leveling the gun at Gino. Travis scrambled to tackle him to the ground. Too late. He fired once.

That's twice I've been thrown to the ground in one day, Gino thought, as he looked up at the starlit sky. He glanced at the moon for a moment to find disappointment that it was only a crescent that night. *I like all or nothing,* he resolved as he lay there. *Full moon or new moon, if the moon half-asses what it does more than half the time, then as humans how can we be expected not to do anything less?*

A second gunshot brought him back to the present. He struggled to sit up and felt the warmth rush down his right shoulder and bicep to spread in several rivulets down his forearm and fall off his fingertips onto the grass lawn. *A shot for a shot, I guess,* he resolved as he noted the knife still sticking out of the struggling Patrick's arm. Wes noticed just then that his enemy was rising, and he snapped out of his delusion to confront the small Italian.

Although still seated, Gino was ready, and he swung his leg under Wes' feet to knock him on the ground and force the air from his lungs for a few seconds. The small Italian struggled to rise, using the strength of his left arm to propel himself clumsily to his feet. Dozens of people from the house party were now out on the lawn, as well. With gaping mouths, they watched in shock and horror what was happening. A couple frat boys were cheering on the scuffle on the ground, as Travis tried to wrestle the gun away from Patrick. But most of the people had already seen the wound Gino carried on his shoulder and knew that this was no simple matter. The girls whom Travis had given the cocaine to in the party were now standing outside, as well. The high remained evident on their distraught faces as they looked on at their new drug dealer handling another form of business.

Travis knocked the gun away and it skidded to a halt near Gino's feet. He would have had it too, but his shoulder screamed in pain as he reached his right hand down to grab it. When he switched positions to pick it up with the left, Wes' own hand shot forth and grabbed the revolver. *Great,* Gino thought, *just when things were looking up.* Wes did not fire at him, but did not hesitate to smack the barrel of the revolver against Gino's face.

Gino hit the ground and turned as Wes leveled the gun at Travis while he was still entangled with Patrick in a mess of limbs and grunts. Wes waited for a moment, trying to get a clear shot, and Gino struggled to get up and shove the gun away before his friend was killed. The third gunshot rang out.

Patrick made no sounds when he died. The bullet went clean through his head and spilled blood and brain all over the

51

lawn and Travis' face. Travis looked to be nearly as stunned as Wes, as he sat there with his own blood mingling with that of his enemy's on his crimson face. He did not even look in Wes' direction.

Wes stood dumbfounded, not even lowering the gun. Screams from the girls all around could not even shake him as he stood staring at his best friend's lifeless face accented by a hole right above his left eye. He shivered for a moment as he stood there, just watching stunned as Gino ripped the knife from Patrick's shoulder. He gathered Travis from off the ground and they both sprinted to their truck. Girls were still screaming, but the sound of a distant siren began to drown their voices out. He snapped into reality and looked at the gun in his hand, and then back to the corpse on the lawn. Red and blue lights played in Patrick's lifeless eyes. Wes took a deep breath and started running.

*

The strain in his leg muscles was almost too much to bear, but Wes kept his steady pace of a full sprint to escape the squad car undoubtedly trailing close behind. He stole a glance over his shoulder and saw the blue and white streaks hit the darkened trees in the neighborhood, growing less and less faint as time drove on. He made his move to the house on his right. A leap over the brick wall and into the backyard gave him a moment of peace. The savage barks of a massive Pit Bull brought Wes' rest to an end, and he found himself running from another sort of trouble and hopping the next wall to enter a back alley behind the central Phoenix neighborhood.

*

Officer Lawrence scanned the trees and shrubbery on either side of the street, as he drove no more than ten miles per hour. His lights were on to reveal what lay in the darkness, with both beams on the top of his patrol car shining in either direction similar to the glowing eyes of an owl scanning for its prey.

"Maggie, I repeat. Three shots fired at the premises on 5th and Thomson. Requesting back up immediately. I am in pursuit. Suspect is on foot and armed," Lawrence said aloud to his dashboard.

"*10-4, Officer Lawrence,*" the voice came back thick with static. "*Two units responding.*"

I hope they hurry, he thought. Although it was a little more than just unorthodox, the officer had allowed his partner to stay behind and wait for the ambulance to arrive at the house. Alone, Lawrence continued on in pursuit of the murderer. Several people at the house party informed him that two additional men had been involved. That explained the inferno that engulfed a vehicle just near to the house, but he had seen no one escape and so figured he would leave them for later. *Maybe this guy knows who they are.*

*

"God damn it!" Wes exclaimed, as he sat with his back against the brick wall of the alley. He tried to stick close to the shadows, but there always seemed to be a little moonlight trickling down on him. His foot twisted badly in the last leap he had made, and when he tried to rise again to begin another sprint, it resulted in a loud crash against three aluminum trashcans blocking his path.

Wes took the revolver from his pocket and examined it. Three bullets left. If the cop had a partner, he would need to have incredible accuracy. *No, I already have my fuckin' best friend's blood on my hands tonight. Do I really need the filthy blood of two pigs on my conscience too?* He cringed at the thought, but silently reserved that perhaps it was for the best.

The young man thought of the others at the party, but more specifically the two men who destroyed his car and got away before he could come to his senses and put bullets into their faces, as well. *It was an accident,* he reassured himself. *That bastard was grappling with Patrick and there was nothing I could do. I aimed... I aimed well.*

Wes punched the wall at the stupidity of his last thought.

"If you had aimed well, Patrick would still be alive and those dumb fucks wouldn't," Wes berated himself in a harsh whisper. "Those fuckin' bastards. They... they're responsible, not me."

Blue and red started washing the brick wall to his right, slowly brightening as the patrol car drew silently nearer, until white beams shot into the alley. Wes ducked behind the trashcans and silently prayed to a God he did not know. The light stayed, as if it was alive itself, ready to spring forth and grab the criminal and haul him off to an eternal prison of guilt and remorse. Wes silently pulled the revolver's hammer back.

That was him, I'm sure of it, Officer Lawrence thought. He subtly shut the door of his squad car. Drawing his handgun, he slowly made his way around the vehicle to the end of the alleyway. Despite the heavy beams of light penetrating the alley's corners, the young man he had just seen was nowhere to be found. Lawrence crept forward, practically on his toes to muffle any sound his clumsy feet might produce.

"It's the police," Lawrence announced loud and deliberate. No response came. "Kid, I'm not going to hurt you, I just need to take you to the station for some questioning."

Still no response. What did I expect? "Okay, Officer, take me in!" Lawrence nearly chuckled at the thought when a crack resonated through the alley that threw him to the pavement. A sharp pain twisted through the left side of his chest, and he instinctively reached to feel the wound. The lead burned his fingers and he pulled his hand away to suck on the singed skin. The vest stopped the bullet from plunging into his chest. The welt that began spreading across his skin underneath his clothes made Lawrence cringe and gasp for breath while he lay on the ground.

Wes used the wall to balance himself as he rose to his feet, peeking over the trashcans to find the policeman lying on the pavement. He patiently waited for another moment to see if there would be another man in blue stepping out of the parked squad car, and when none came, he started to make his way out of the alley.

A soft moan protruded from the policeman's mouth. Wes

immediately tried to slink back into the shadows. His feet betrayed him and he tripped over one of the trashcans to come down hard on his backside. The officer rose to a crouched position but kept a short distance between himself and the trashcans. One hand clutched his throbbing chest. The other held his handgun out in the young man's direction.

Wes put his revolver atop the trashcan directly before him and fired once in the officer's direction, only to have his shot uselessly bury into the police car's fender. A gunshot came in response to his own, the policeman's bullet shredding through his fingers and tendons to nearly rip his hand in two. Wes screamed in agony and dropped the gun onto his lap, cursing himself for wasting the second-to-the-last bullet.

Terrible aim, terrible aim, he could have screamed at himself. *That's twice in one fuckin' night that my bullets haven't gone where I wanted.* Wes wiped away the tears. Were they shed for Patrick or himself? He peeked out at the officer.

"You're a young man," Lawrence was saying. "Don't do this. Your life does not have to end this way if you just put the gun down, kid."

He doesn't sound like a liar, at least, Wes thought as he cradled his disfigured hand. He looked out toward the officer, now visible from the cracks of light between the trashcans. The man in blue was less than ten feet away, weapon drawn as he searched out his wounded prey. The revolver was heavy then, four pounds exaggerated with the burden of the night, and shined with the light of the half-moon above.

C'mon, kid. Please don't make me kill you. Lawrence's heart wrenched at the idea. People make bad decisions all the time. Sure, murder was a stretch, but maybe this kid had more on his plate than any other cop would give him credit for. What kind of home life would drive someone to such violence? He kept his gun leveled at the trashcans, just a couple yards away now. He could see everything, and hear the terrified heavy breathing of the young criminal. Lawrence wondered if he should have waited in the car for his backup, but then decided he had done the right thing. Nevertheless, his heart beat heavily into his mind with deep resonating thuds accented by the raspy breaths of the young man behind the trashcans.

"C'mon, kid," Officer Lawrence said. "Just put the weapon down. I'll get you to a hospital and everything'll be fine. I promise."

The breathing continued. What started as quick rasping draws for breath shifted into drawn-out inhalations spaced few and far between. Lawrence began the final turn around the last trashcan when a crack of gunfire echoed through the alley and his vision filled with grey smoke. The officer raised his gun again and checked his body with his other hand to find that not a single wound resided there. *No... my God, no.*

Burnt powder permeated the atmosphere and wisps of smoke could still be seen rising on the other side of that last trashcan. Lawrence crept up and found the young man's body slumped against the brick wall. The revolver was still in the firm grip of his lifeless hand resting against his outer thigh.

Fresh blood spread along the bricks like a spider's web. The criminal's face was nearly unrecognizable with the mask of dark crimson still flowing in struggled pumps from the top of his cranium.

Betrayal

The store on the street's corner was basic. Red and white paint covered the brick walls in a striped pattern. It had service pumps so there was a possibility of a great amount of money to be had there, but Max felt nervous about the whole venture. *Who the hell pays for gas with cash anymore?* he wondered. Max turned to the man seated next to him. Todd was in the driver's seat, as usual, wearing a dark jacket and pants and keeping his shaved head exposed. Despite the darkness outside, a faint gleam of moonlight still shone off Todd's scalp.

"Get in there; let's go," Todd said impatiently.

"I just," Max started, "P-people don't usually…"

"I already told you, everything is fine. I know the kid who works in there, it's not even something you should be worrying about," Todd explained calmly. With a twist of his mouth he added, "Now, get in there."

"Damn it," Max muttered as he opened the door.

He started toward the store and looked back to the car. Todd was drumming his fingers on the steering wheel and rocking his head back and forth violently to some song. He must have sensed Max's eyes. Todd shot him a look and mouthed "now." Max grunted and shook his head softly before turning back to the gas station.

*

Samuel ran a damp cloth along the counter, preferring to keep himself busy during his long shifts at the register. Hardly anyone came in at one in the morning. It was a wonder to him why the store was even open, because it was nowhere near a highway that would be supplying gas to those who needed it so late. Even still, the store was open and he ran the cloth in small circles that helped to lift water and coffee stains from the red counter.

A small bell rang as someone stepped inside the store. Samuel did not look up for a moment and just kept working. *When they need me, they'll say so,* he thought. He continued his cleaning for a few more seconds, until the silence became awkward and he looked up. A man dressed in all black and wearing a ski mask leveled a handgun to his face. Samuel's heart doubled its pace and his breath quickened. *Another great night at the corner store,* he thought with a sigh. *Maybe it's just this neighborhood.*

"The r-register," Max said. "Open it, n-now."

Samuel did as he was told. As he dug through the slots and brought out the twenties and tens, he looked up at the brown eyes cut into the ski mask, "You know it's pretty pointless to rob a corner store. We never really keep more than a couple hundred at a time."

"J-just shut up and put the money in this bag," Max replied. He shoved an empty potato sack in the cashier's face. "Unless you h-have money somewhere else in this f-fuckin' store."

"Nope, the manager comes at midnight and takes it all

away," Samuel lied, while trying to hide a smirk.

"Oh," Max said. He continuously looked away to the front of the store, where Todd waited. Samuel took his time in the hopes of someone else coming in, but as he stuck the last single into the bag, he was still alone with the robber.

With the sack filled up, Max turned to leave when a glass jug of donation coins smashed against the back of his head. He was out cold, sprawled against the tiled flooring of the corner store amongst a dazzling array of pennies, nickels, dimes, and quarters. Samuel looked from the unconscious man on the floor and back to his own hands with a nervous chuckle. Carefully he pulled the handgun from the man's fruitless grasp and laid it on the counter. Tires screeching outside indicated the gunman's ride made it away, but Samuel did not care in the slightest.

*

"Son, all you have to do is tell us who put you up to it and you're lookin' at a shorter sentence... you know, once your court date an' all that gets settled," the bearded detective informed Max from across the table. Max eyed the cop up and down. A maroon tie sat loosely about his neck and his cheap blazer was thrown haphazardly on the back of his seat. It was going to be a long night.

His head was still throbbing and he rubbed it then, trying to wave away the pain that came from the sudden pressure of a ten-pound jar. He sighed. There was no way that he could implicate Todd's involvement in the robbery, or else he would be killed. Todd's connections appeared unlimited and Max almost gagged at the realization that he himself had been one of those connections on more than one occasion. If not on the streets before the court date was even final, then somewhere in prison, a sharp edge would find his stomach.

"I was there by myself," Max stated.

"The cashier seems to believe that there was someone waiting in the parking lot for you, but they left as soon as things didn't go your way," the detective replied. "Now, you don't want to lie to us, son. Just tell us what happened and things could go a lot better for you."

"I was there by myself," Max said again. His stomach turned and he felt saliva building in his mouth. He fought back the urge to vomit by taking a deep breath.

"All right, all right, for now that's fine I guess," the detective said. "What about the cashier; did you know him?"

"No," Max lied.

"He said he recognized your face when he took the ski mask off, but couldn't place who you were," the detective said. "You're sure you don't know him, son?"

"Don't I get a phone call or something? I should t-talk to my lawyer before talking to you guys directly, I think, right?" Max asked. He looked to his right in the cramped white room. A silver mirror hung on the wall. He knew from movies and television shows that he watched that people were behind that glass, observing the way he answered questions and taking notes on what he said. The reflection he saw in the mirror was enough to make him cry, but he held the tears back from the teenage boy who looked back at him while seated at the table with a cop. He was thin, almost gangly, with brown eyes that looked more like they belonged to a ten-year-old than someone considered a man by law. His beard was scraggly and sporadic, as if his face could not decide on whether or not it wanted to grow up or not.

"You'll have a lawyer appointed to you by the state, because you don't have one yourself; we already looked into all that. Your parents have been notified about what's happened. I gotta' tell you... they didn't seem all that surprised about it. Even still, they said they'll post your bail in a couple days," the detective said. He paused in the hopes of getting some emotion out of the kid. Nothing. "They must really love you. That's not a cheap bail to post... maybe they have some money saved up for just such an occasion, huh? Maybe they will find you a lawyer... but they ain't gonna' be able to brush *everything* under the rug."

Max felt nervous as thoughts rushed into his head. Even if he was not back out in Phoenix for a bit, Todd would not believe that he stayed silent. He would know by now that he was in a police station, and he would assume he ratted on him. *He's always treated me like shit anyway,* Max resolved. He wanted to scream and beg the cop to tell him what to do. He clenched his eyelids shut for a moment and the officer's deep voice shoved through his thoughts.

"I just don't get it, son. Things will be a lot better for everyone if you just start tellin' the truth."

LOVE

There was barely anywhere a person could look and not see black. Dark gray clouds were gathered overhead and brought their own tears to mingle with those of the people standing all around the hole in the ground. Jennifer's own saltwater fell lazily to patter with the sprinkling rain on the burgundy wood six feet beneath her. She looked up to find the priest going on about the youth's life and who he was, from what he had heard from the deceased's mother and brother. He never once mentioned his death, only life was worth mentioning in those final moments before the first dirt would be thrown and the coffin covered in earth.

Jennifer sighed and gave a gentle sob at the loss, though she was not completely certain why. She felt for the boy, but did not know him as well as she might have, and so her tears were somewhat inexplicable. His mother was a wreck across the hole in the ground, weeping bitterly and wringing her hands in a handkerchief soaked through with rain, snot, and tears. The priest continued with a small prayer, hoping that the youth's soul would be carried into the good graces of God, the Father, and that the angels would watch him along his final journey.

To Jennifer's left stood the boy's brother. He was barely recognizable to her, although she knew him more than well. Samuel's normally clean-shaven cheeks had the dark shadow of a beard that resulted from days without shaving, and his hair was tousled, despite the fact that she thought she remembered him doing it nicely that morning. He had no tears. No water would flow from his brown eyes, and they just stared sullenly down at the casket that would be the only thing holding his brother from then on. She grabbed his hand, berating herself at the same time that she thanked God, or whatever other force there was in the world, that it was not him in the ground.

*

Jennifer woke with a start. Sweat beaded along the surface of her skin, and she looked wearily at the young man lying next to her. He was sleeping soundly, or as soundly as he could sleep. He was just now becoming accustomed to sleep without cocaine withdrawals that had been plaguing his body for a while. After a failed attempt at going back to sleep, she decided to touch her lover's shoulder and roust him from his dreams.

Samuel looked groggy as he gathered his bearings. "What's wrong, hun?"

"I had a nightmare…" Jennifer started, feeling stupid as she said the words.

"What happened?" he asked, trying to sound as if he cared, while keeping his eyes closed and searching for that dream he had lost.

"Your brother had…" she began, then choked on her words, as if they were true. "I don't know. It was so real. He had died."

"He's right there," Samuel replied as he pointed

nonchalantly in his brother's direction on the other side of the room. It was true, and Jason slumbered there in his twin bed with a look of contentment on his bruised and swollen face. "He's not going to die. He came out of the coma and everything is going to be fine. He just needs a little more sleep than everyone else." Samuel chuckled. "That doesn't mean that he's going to sleep forever."

"Sorry I brought it up," Jennifer said with a tone of irritation.

"Ah, what did I do?" Samuel asked as he opened his eyes to gaze into hers.

"Nothing. I just wish that you would listen to me sometimes," she answered.

"I listen all the time, hun," Samuel protested. He sat up in the bed and stared into her gray eyes for a while before he smiled deep. "You're beautiful."

"Oh, jeez," she said with a smile. He was still smiling broad and her heart fluttered at the sight of it. His smile did that to her, making her body tremble in eager anticipation for another kiss.

"I'm so glad you're in my—" he began, but was cut short by a light tapping on the front door of his apartment. "Jesus, what fuckin' time is it?"

"Two-thirty," Jennifer answered, a look of anxiety set plainly on her face. Her thick lips curled downward, and her brow furrowed slightly when she looked in the direction of the knocking. Almost like she could see through the walls. Who could be there so late?

"Stay here," Samuel said, as he rose from bed. Rubbing a slight ache from his right shoulder he strode through the bedroom doorway and out into a living room cluttered with books.

Samuel stopped just short of the door and grabbed the wooden baseball bat propped against the corner. Leaning in, he took a glance through the peephole and nearly jumped back when he saw that Max, the same youth who attempted robbery at the corner store just days before, stood on the other side. The lanky young man looked nervous and constantly glanced over both shoulders. Samuel decided there was really no exit from the confrontation, and so tightened his fingers around the base of the bat and kept peering through the peephole.

"What do you want?" Samuel asked harshly from the other side of the door.

"Oh, Sam, thank God you're here," Max began. "Let me c-come in and talk to you for a minute."

"What the fuck for?"

"I'm having a huge problem. I n-need your help."

"After what you tried to do just days ago?" Samuel could have laughed, if he did not fear the possibility of Max having a blade or gun in his pocket.

"It's about Todd, and it involves you, t-too," Max stated.

Samuel turned about and saw Jennifer standing in the bedroom doorway. He motioned for her to go back into the room and she was reluctant initially, but after a brief glare from her lover, she slunk back into the bedroom's shadows. The youth opened the door cautiously, gripping the bat's handle, as he stared defiantly into Max's teary brown eyes.

"What is it?" Samuel asked.

"Let me come inside, please," Max said with another glance over his shoulder to the parking lot. "Please, Sam."

"You do anything stupid I'll put a dent in your head so deep the cops won't know which mouth you talked shit out of," Samuel stated with a savage tone. "Got it?"

"Got it," Max said as he edged his way into the apartment. The lanky youth glanced around at the place and shrugged as if to say it looked better than his. He sat in a wicker chair that served as a piece of Samuel's indoor furniture, and stared at the floor for a short time, while Samuel stood still clutching the bat close to his chest. He closed the door and locked it.

"Keep your voice down too, my brother's asleep and my woman's in the other room," Samuel said.

"I turned in Todd when the cops asked me who put me up to robbing your g-gas station," Max began. Samuel stayed silent as the tall youth continued. "They've already l-linked him to his boss, James, and they will move soon on their whole operation."

"I'm not familiar with their whole operation, so you'll have to enlighten me," Samuel replied as he eased his weapon to a more relaxed position on the ground.

"The reason that Todd put your brother in the hospital was b-because of a huge loss in money recently, and he took that out on you two. I guess because you've never really d-done anything in retaliation before. Todd's a f-fuckin' bully. If he thinks he can get away with it then he does whatever he wants," Max explained. "He was rash and stupid, yeah, but he has a f-few cronies and is associated with some people of power in Phoenix that can cause trouble for more than just a seventeen-year-old kid and his older brother. There's two s-sides in the struggle for money in this fuckin' city, and he's also under the impression that you blew him off to buy your coke from that guy Jacob. You do know about the t-two sides, right?"

"I'm sure there's more than two. There's probably over a dozen gangs and stupid fucks trying to pull the same shit you guys do; you just see yourselves as rivals I'm guessing... Still don't see what it has to do with me." Samuel shrugged. "I paid off the debts I owed to him."

"That doesn't matter. You're friends with p-people that are on the other side," Max said. "Zach's boys. Jacob is one of the hired people under Zach, and runs his own bullshit, just as Todd is a hired fucker under James, running his own bullshit. I don't know exactly w-what's happening with Zach's boys, because as far as I know they've been pretty clean for a while and haven't fucked up in terms of the law. After the c-cops pulled out everything they wanted me to tell them about James though... I can tell you that Todd and his boys will go looking for anyone that they think squealed. I may be the first p-person he'd think of, but I came to you because you're the second."

"What are you suggesting?"

"How long have you b-been out of the loop?" Max inquired.

"What do you mean?" Samuel asked, almost irritated.

"Jacob's buddies, Steve and Frank, were killed by four of Todd's guys, j-just a few days ago. Right after Jay Stanson's funeral," Max explained, picking at his lower lip. Samuel looked to the ground for a moment in silence. Max continued, "Steve and Frank w-were avenged by another pair of guys who I haven't heard of, though. No one knows their names, or if they do, they aren't giving up the information. Whoever these guys were, though, they were either involved or are directly responsible for the d-deaths of two guys named Wes and Patrick. That's two of the guys I needed to take out already bumped off, so I only need to d-deal with the other two and Todd, and then I'll be safe. Those five are the only ones w-who know about me working for Todd. Then I can l-leave and not have to look back."

"Wait a minute. You want to kill Todd and two of his cronies?" Samuel was baffled. He shook his head.

"Sam?" Jennifer's voice said behind him. She stood in the doorway again, this time wearing one of his shirts to cover up any skin that Max might look at. Her delicate features were filled with anxiety. Anxiety caused by him, not for the first time. "Sam what are you two talking about?"

"Nothing," Sam said brusquely. "It's nothing, hun. Can you wait in the other room?"

"No," she said matter-of-factly. "I'm fine right here."

Samuel looked back at Max and bit the inside of his cheek. "Todd and his men?"

"Yes," Max replied calmly. "I can't run from this shit until they're dead or in prison… And, with as long as it's taking the cops to process this shit, then I'm going to h-have to go with 'dead'."

Samuel became nervous then, and tensed his fingers around the bat's handle. "Why aren't you still in jail, anyway?"

"Innocent 'til proven guilty shit, but they will prove me guilty," Max explained. "My family has some money and they were able to bail me out… I'm grateful, but, I'm fucked if I don't get outta' here. I'm leaving town as soon as we're done with what we have to do tonight. I don't know where I'll go, but I can't stay here."

"We?"

"Don't you get it, Samuel?" Max started to get agitated. "There's no way that any cop would expect you to have participated in any conflict since you never reported a name when you brought Jason in to the hospital; so you're clean on that end. On the other end, once the cops start clamping down on everyone, your name and mine are going to be drawn headfirst into the list of potential narks. I need your help."

"I don't know…" Samuel said. His stomach felt likely to cave in on itself. Just the thought of killing another human being, good or bad, was nearly enough to make him vomit.

"Sam," Jennifer said. Her mouth was agape and her gray eyes would not leave his. "How can you even *think* about this?"

71

"Look what Todd did to your brother," Max said.

Samuel closed his eyes. Todd's former associate was right. There was no way that he could let that disrespect to his brother and his family go unnoticed. Something had to be done. Samuel wanted nothing more than to go and hold her, but there were more important things to take care of.

"When?" Samuel asked his guest.

Max stood and stretched his legs for a moment. "Now."

Samuel took a deep breath. "Okay."

Jennifer crumpled to the floor as soon as she heard her boyfriend was willing to go. She pleaded and begged him not to leave and put his life in such reckless danger. He reassured her using his most calm voice that was still unable to quell the feelings of emotion in her belly, or the tears welling in her eyes.

"Please don't go, Sam, please," Jennifer begged.

Samuel waved Max to wait outside and the lanky youth left the apartment to light a cigarette right outside the door. He turned to his girlfriend. "Everything's going to be fine, hun. Don't be so worried all the time."

"I just, I..."

"Don't say it," Samuel said with a sad smile. Placing his hand on her stomach he added, "You barely even know me. It's just the fact that we're sharing something special with one another. Don't say it, okay?"

She nodded and tried once more to stop the flow of tears and depression that plagued her mind and body. He gave her one last kiss on the forehead before standing up to leave.

Jennifer sat there on the unkempt carpet for what felt like minutes already, listening to the sound of the door close and the lock slide into place. She didn't care that she barely knew him. She knew enough to know exactly how she felt, whether it was because of the life growing inside her or not. Her heart felt ravaged when she gathered herself up to go back to lie restlessly on the bed. Her gaze caught a glimpse of an older picture of Sam, his brother, and their mother hanging on the wall. She looked into his sad eyes, in spite of the smile he forced.

"I love you," she whispered.

Death

Max flung open the trunk of his car and exposed his arsenal to the young man at his side. Samuel cringed in disappointment to find that his partner only had a pair of nightsticks and a newly purchased set of kitchen knives.

"You have got to be fucking kidding me," Samuel started.

Max threw him a harsh look. Sam didn't seem to notice. He stared to his right down the darkened street, only illuminated with small patches of light from the streetlamps. The apartment building just to the right of Max's car looked corroded, like a gust of wind could topple the entire complex over and those inside would be buried under aged dust. Samuel's brown eyes flicked back and forth from the apartments and to his partner. Max kept a stern look of intent while sliding the knives individually and with caution into his pockets.

Once Max was finished he took a deep breath of Phoenix's polluted air. "Let's have a s-smoke."

Samuel smacked his pack against the palm of his hand a couple times and threw a cigarette between his lips as if he was going to eat it. Max took the one offered to him and they stood briefly in waiting for the small flame that would calm their nerves. When Samuel took his first drag, it seemed nearly instantaneous that his body relaxed. He closed his eyes and ears to the world. He forgot about the problems that clouded his life, just as age, pollution and apathy had corroded the apartment complex to his right.

"You sure about this?" Max asked. "Once we go in there... there isn't any b-backing o—"

"I got that," Samuel replied. Taking a longer drag than normal, he stared down the street for another moment. "I'm sure. I thought y-you were sure, too."

"Oh, I'm sure," Max said. His voice cracked, exposing his artificial confidence.

The cigarettes went by quickly, too quickly, and so the pair waited until after the second and third smokes before finally vamping up the courage to walk inside that dreaded building. Max led the way, using a crude lock pick to get past the initial barrier that took the form of the complex's front gate. The lock was easy enough to pass, after a profuse amount of swear words and jiggling the doorknob, but the two young men were well on their way before long.

I hate stairs, Max thought. He glared down at the steps beneath his feet. The wood creaked and echoed through the complex with each step the lanky youth and his shorter companion took. They reached the top of the staircase and stopped for a moment on the second floor, so Max could gather his bearings. He glanced around the hallway until he found the dirty brass numbers next to the doors. Content with himself, the lanky youth started walking slowly down the hallway, as his hand slipped into his front pocket.

"What number did you s—" Samuel began.

"Shh!" Max cut him short with an exaggerated glare from his dark eyes.

215, 215, Max repeated silently to keep himself from going insane. *211, 213... 215.* His breath stopped short, as he stared at the door. Immediately he began to feel a sense of regret growing in his belly. He searched down either side of the hallway for an escape into something, anything, better than where he was. They had gone at a good time, he decided. It was barely past three in the morning and there had been literally no passersby as they walked down the hallway. Few cars were on the road. The less witnesses the better, and from what he could tell there wouldn't be a soul to tell anyone what they saw that night. His hand fumbled at the knives in his pocket until he felt one of the blades bite him and he instinctively put his finger in his mouth.

"Use the pick," Samuel urged, with a whisper barely audible to an insect.

"Shh," Max said with irritation. *How many times do I have to get this guy to shut the fuck up?* He ran his hand through his dark hair and then, shaking, drew the lock pick from the left pocket of his jeans.

Each click the pick made, as it passed another individual barrier in the doorknob, was equivalent to the loudest racket that Max had ever heard. The sounds even took on distinct noises. When the metal grated against itself, a yell of "Run!" penetrated the air around him. As the bars locked into place, a gruff "Kill" sounded in the darkness. Max wiped the sweat from his brow with his left hand and finally slid the last locking bar into place.

The door had a slight creak to it, and despite the fact that it was nothing like the stairs they had just traversed, the sound seemed much more exaggerated and frightening. As he entered the apartment, Max slid the lock pick back into his left pocket and stuffed his hand into the right one to find a knife. There were several in there, so it did not come as too much of a shock when he sliced open a finger. He drew one of the serrated blades and peered through the blackness of an empty living room. Samuel held back in the threshold, pulling the nightstick from his jeans and closing the door so that only a crack remained for the pair to escape quickly.

Tucker was a young man under thirty but somehow had already started balding. The gangster's job's stress may have left him without a thick head of hair but it never affected his sleep. He slumbered soundly in his room with a secretive grin set plainly on his grim features. Max tiptoed over to his bed and looked at the sleeping face. A sense of calm blanketed the young man's room, yet what Max was about to do would destroy any piece of that and leave it dark and dismal. *He looks peaceful,* Max thought for a moment as he stared down at Tucker. *No, no.* He shook his head in an attempt to knock out any stupidity. *This mother fucker would kill you, too, as soon as he had the chance. He'd kill you now if he knew you were here. Wait, who wouldn't? Fuck it all, the bastard can't live. He'll kill you as soon as Todd gives the order. Now, just… one deep slice.*

Max's hand quivered and the blade appeared to blur when he brought it closer to Tucker's neck. Tucker stayed in the same position, staring at the back of his eyelids as if some movie played there meant only for him. Once the cold steel touched his neck and began to draw across it, the eyelids flung open and he instantly went for Max's throat with one hand while another grappled at his own.

"What the fuck are you doing?" Tucker shouted.

A thin line of blood formed around his gullet, and Tucker nearly laughed at Max's attempt at murder. His smirk died when Max knocked his hand away, pushing him down on the bed and bringing the knife whirring down to slam into his chest. Tucker knew that was no paper cut. The blade had found its way between his ribs and punched into his lung, but a sense of numbing spread through his body like he was already linked to an IV filled with Novocain. He struggled against his slender opponent, throwing his elbows into Max's face and filling his vision with tears, but still the blade slammed down again.

"Holy fuck," Samuel said as he stood in the doorway. He saw the struggle and was unable to move for a second. Tucker's desperation fueled him, though. *If only just to put this poor bastard out of his misery,* Samuel thought with a twisted stomach. The nightstick came down three times. Each shot hammering Tucker's forehead with a ghastly blow, until he slipped into unconsciousness.

The pair stood above their victim with uncertainty. Samuel took a step back. It was plain to see that he would have

78

nothing more to do with that murder. Max eyed him down, but only for a second. This was his plan anyway. He slid the knife across his enemy's throat with some actual force, drawing the life out of Tucker with fading pumps of crimson.

*

"I'm just telling you what I 'eard," Alex said with agitation into the phone. In his early twenties, Alex was of stocky build and medium height. In spite of his average appearance, he had a short amount of patience and an attitude problem beyond resolution. His friend on the other end replied briefly, and Alex did not even bother to answer before pressing the off button and tossing the telephone into his dilapidated couch.

Alex pulled the hammer of his revolver back into position as he walked back into his bedroom. He glanced over his shoulder for a moment, as if a shadow would spring forth and put a knife into his heart. With the gun securely resting on his nightstand, Alex laid down in bed once more and stared at the open doorway into the dimly-lit hallway. He snorted irritation with himself and ran a hand through his black hair to calm himself. His eyes began to droop, taking him back to sleep without much fuss, other than the phone call he had made just minutes before.

A shadow passed in front of his dreary eyes that drew him from slumber. Alex's hand shot out to grab the revolver, but found it already gone. Once his eyes adjusted, he found an unfamiliar youth standing over the left side of his bed and Max, Todd's most recent hire, lurking on the right. They each held a nightstick, and the bludgeons that rained down on his head shook the sleep off him, before sucking all the energy from his limbs. He tumbled from his bed. Alex did not even feel the knife wounds, but could see the lack of passion in the shorter youth's brown eyes when Max's butcher knife rushed forward into Alex's heart.

What a confusing feeling, Alex thought while he leaned over into his nightstand. Exhaustion crept into his body as he saw the two figures suddenly become unintelligible shadows and depart the room. His heart worked frantically in his chest to produce a beat for every five seconds, then every six or seven, then every ten, until it seemed like it begged to be able to beat at least twice a minute. He went to sleep.

*

"All right, that's enough," Samuel said. There was a distorted look of agony on his face. He looked into the bathroom mirror and cringed.

"We have to kill Todd," Max replied dryly.

Samuel thought about it for a moment. He looked frightened and yet invigorated at the same time. His stomach was made entirely out of knots. "I just... I don't know."

"What is there to know?" the lanky youth at his side asked as he finished washing his hands. "The bastard n-needs to die more than anyone else in this situation. We have to kill him. There's no backing out now. His two remaining cronies are dead now, and when he f-finds out about that, he'll erupt like a fuckin' volcano. He probably has hordes of m-money stashed up and can hire a dozen men to track Alex and Tucker's killers."

"No, because he didn't hire anyone to track the two guys who killed Patrick and Wes," Samuel argued. As he said it, he knew his voice showed no willpower, and he knew the argument was fruitless but still he tried.

"Not yet," Max answered.

They both walked casually out of the bathrooms and strode down the complex's hallway to emerge back out onto the street to their waiting car. Samuel craved a cigarette more than he had in his entire life, but a passerby quickly made him decide that he should wait until they were safely away from the complex. Once Alex's body was found, there was no telling how much evidence the police would need to be hot on him and Max's trail. *No, no, we didn't leave any evidence,* Samuel tried to reassure himself. The weapons had all been taken with them, and once the deeds were done they would be burnt and tossed along with the clothes on their backs. The car started with a jump and a sputter and it took mere seconds for Max to launch it down the street.

Samuel lit a cigarette and looked morosely out the passenger window. "Do you think Todd is up?"

"It doesn't matter," Max answered with a shrug.

"How can that not matter?" Samuel asked. He took in a long drag of smoke.

"We have this n-now," Max replied. He pulled Alex's gun from his pocket and showed the youth seated next to him the

81

intricacy of the weapon. Samuel appeared to be in awe. He gazed at the dark gray metal that would make their next victim so much easier.

"You don't think we're doing the wrong thing here, do you?" Samuel wondered aloud.

Max shook his head in annoyance. Without responding, he turned on the radio and changed the station. Hip-hop started blaring through Max's cheap speakers and shook the old vehicle so much Samuel thought pieces were likely to fall off. The youth stared out the window again at the buildings and parks passing to his right. Nighttime enveloped Phoenix like a shroud that assured every individual calm was in the air. There were a couple hours before morning traffic would hit and people would begin going to work.

They needed to hurry.

The final house was a little better than a shack, but not by much. Todd's abode was bought with blood and drug money, and because he had no other job, it was unlikely that the cocaine dealer would be anywhere else. Samuel glanced from the grey home and back to his partner, sitting in the driver's seat. Max checked time and again, to make certain the revolver was loaded, wishing that he had fired a weapon at least once before moving to end someone's life with it.

"Let's g-go," Max finally decided.

Samuel reluctantly climbed out of the vehicle and pushed his exhausted legs forward to the house. It was quiet on Todd's street. Not a single house was illuminated inside, and those with their fronts lit were dim from the sorry excuses for streetlamps that lined the neighborhood. The two young men walked uneasily to the front door and Max drew the lock pick from his pocket, once again. Samuel glanced over his shoulder to ensure no one was watching, his gaze lingering on his car sitting in the front lawn like a trophy for all to see.

After several failed attempts on the front door they both moved swiftly and silently to the back gate. Its rusty hinges squealed in protest as they opened it, but the world came back to stillness once they were in Todd's backyard. Weeds had overgrown his shrubbery and the lawn was a dying yellow. Samuel had to suppress a nervous chuckle at the pathetic house and its surroundings. *If Todd is supposed to be such a big-timer then why is he living in such a shit heap neighborhood? Living here he could easily get away with an audit, that's for sure. Or maybe he's just all talk, no money.* Samuel supposed that maybe it was a bit of both. Todd would have trouble with the IRS if he had a bunch of nice vehicles and a mansion, to boot. Regardless, any place would be better than this one.

The back door refused to open to Max's quivering fingers and so they both looked at one another for what to do for longer than a moment. There was not much else to do and so Samuel walked into the yard for a second before returning with a hefty brick in his right hand. As quietly as he could, he smashed the glass above the patio door's knob. Showers of invisible warnings clattered to the tile flooring of Todd's home.

Max reached inside and twisted the doorknob, allowing

his partner and him to walk inside unnoticed. Samuel studied his surroundings, from the grimy carpet that stretched nearly throughout the entire house to the failing patio furniture that served as Todd's places of relaxation. The refrigerator was littered with all sorts of papers, the latest being an eviction notice that Todd had aptly wrote "Fuck you!" on.

"All right, let's get this—"

Two gunshots interrupted Max. He grabbed his right knee with one hand, while his other went to his lower belly. As his partner writhed in pain on the ground, Samuel snatched the revolver from his extended hand and shrank into the darkness. He squatted beside a lawn chair for what seemed like an eternity. He could hear Todd's combat boots slide off the dirty carpet and onto the kitchen tile. What began as a quiet laugh reverberated and grew louder throughout the house. Samuel stayed where he was, but could practically see the entire scene played out. The skinhead drug dealer moving swiftly to Max's side, grinning enthusiastically as he realized that he escaped death.

"Oh God, oh God, oh God," Max stammered through the blood in his teeth.

"You are a dumb fuck, aren't you?" Todd's voice replied. He sounded excited. "What the hell were you thinking, breaking into my place? Ahhh... Maybe Alex was right about hearing some shit in his house. Did you go there, too, you scrawny fuck?"

Todd kicked Max swiftly in the belly, driving pain out in

startled gasps and sobs. Todd laughed and looked around the room. Samuel ducked behind the chair farther, to escape being seen.

"I know you're there, York," Todd announced. "I've been watching your dumbass from the moment you broke my fucking window. You two make quite a bit of noise for a couple of assassins." He chuckled, once again. "Step out and fight me now, you little fuck. I'll even put the gun aside and let you take the first swing. C'mon, let's do it."

He doesn't know, Samuel realized. He stared down at the revolver in his shaking hands. He stood fully, keeping the gun behind the lawn chair and staring with heavy defiance into Todd's unforgiving eyes. The dealer was true to his word. That much could be said of him. He laid his .40 caliber handgun on his kitchen table and moved away from Max, to stand in the moonlight of the room. He probably had shaved his head that night, as it had a particular sheen in the light. It gave his scowl a menacing look as he glared at his former customer. His skin was tight around his face making him appear peculiarly skeletal. Todd was shirtless, and although nearly as lanky as Max, it was obvious that he was coursed with sinewy muscle.

"You put my brother in the hospital," Samuel said, his voice cracking in the process.

"Now's your chance to get revenge," Todd replied. "C'mon, you little faggot, have at it."

A flurry of memories streamed into Samuel's mind as he stood there staring at the drug dealer. The punch he had received several days earlier, the withdrawals he went through because of Todd's cocaine, his brother coming out of his coma and into a confused consciousness, Jennifer's terrified eyes as she had woken in the middle of the night to tell him of a horrific dream involving his brother's funeral. And now Max, slumped in a growing pool of blood and either unwilling or unable to move. Samuel raised the revolver and leveled it at Todd's chest. The look on the dealer's flabbergasted face could have been the funniest thing Samuel had ever seen. He thought he was so clever, having seen the two young men enter his house and shooting one of them, but he had not thought that they might carry any weaponry more powerful than a few kitchen knives or brass knuckles.

Before he could reach toward the kitchen table and grab his weapon again, Samuel fired. Three successive shots collided with Todd's exposed chest and mangled the flesh. Each bullet tore through his back, spraying blood all over the kitchen tile before the drug dealer could even react. Seconds seemed like years as the man turned into a corpse, slumped lifelessly against the kitchen counter, his three gaping wounds spewing crimson life down his belly.

Samuel ran to Max.

"I'm so sorry," Samuel York said to the body in front of him. He used the edge of his shirt to rub small circles around the metal of the pistol in his hand, making sure he handled the barrel and trigger first and foremost, before placing it in Max's. "I'm so sorry."

Max stared at the ceiling with apathetic eyes. Samuel closed his partner's eyelids with reserved silence and looked back to Todd, still gawking incredulous into the darkness of his house. He absently thought about the cops when they would find this scene. Was wiping the prints off enough? Or would they know there was another person involved in the bloody affair. *No time to dwell on it,* Samuel resolved. He rose to his feet and sprinted out the back door.

POWER

The warehouse was faintly lit by the orange glow of only a few lamps. Zach stood in front of his men, informing them on the situation. Several men had recently been killed, including a couple of his own, but even more of his enemy James'. José glanced from side to side at the people they had gathered.

What a ragged bunch, José thought. *Only seven of us came to Zach's call, and this is the most important time.*

"James is weakened now," Zach was saying. "So long as we strike, then there's nothing that will stop us from prevailing with our sales. New drugs have already increased because of the connections we got in Mesa, and the word of mouth Travis has developed."

One of the black men in the small grouping spoke up. José had never seen him before, but his friend Malcolm had been loosely affiliated with Zach's crew for a couple years. "What if we just struck up a deal wit' 'em? There's no sense in killin' all those fuckers, if we can just push 'em out the game."

"James is resilient," Zach began. The confusion on Malcolm's friend's face made him sigh. "He'll keep coming back," the annoyed leader clarified. "We need to eliminate him at the least, and then the rest of his men will fend for themselves on what's to be done."

The warehouse door creaked open then, and everyone in the room looked like deer caught in headlights as they reached for the pistols at their waists.

"Hold on, hold on," José threw up his arms. "It's just a kid."

"What the hell you doin' here, lil' man?" Malcolm asked. The African-American man looked menacing. He had big eyes that sat in dark sunken pits of his gaunt face. Corn rows pulled his hair taut to his head and scruff showed in patches on his cheeks and chin. He stood there with his right hand resting on the handle of his weapon, as if it was the pommel of a sword.

"My name's Jason York," the kid began. "I heard you guys needed some help."

"This is no place for a child," Zach replied with a sigh.

Jason's response was to simply pull a revolver from his pocket. The eight men grabbed at their weapons, again, but José called them off once more and looked with confusion at the young man standing in front of them.

"I came prepared," Jason explained. "I just want to help. Todd and his asshole cronies fucked me up real bad recently, and my brother…" They all waited for additional commentary but the kid held his tongue for a moment. "Todd and all them are gone now, but I realize that James and his friends are just as deadly as that bastard ever was. If you'll let me, I can come with you and help. Think about it."

"It doesn't sound like you are," José answered with the agreement of the rest of them.

"Six more bullets in your crew will do some good," Jason replied matter-of-factly.

"Listen, lil' man; we got no need for another corpse in this bullshit, so just go back to your mama's house and eat some dinner," Malcolm said. The others chuckled nervously, but he gave them a savage stare from his amber eyes and they were silenced. "I'm serious, kid. Go home."

"I..." Jason started.

The sounds of cars outside brought them all out of the silence and they scratched their heads nervously. José moved past the youth and stared out of one of the shutters into the street. Three cars were unloading four men each, and each one of them cocked a pistol hammer back as they gave one another nervous glances.

"Fuck," José said.

"Everyone get in the shadows," Zach ordered.

The men followed his command, retreating to the darkness of the warehouse's corners. Jason followed Malcolm to a corner himself, fumbling at the revolver in his hand to cock the hammer back as the warehouse's door was kicked in.

"We know you fucks are here. Your cars are all outside so you can cut this horseshit and come out of hiding!" James exclaimed. The tall man passed between the first men who had gone through the rickety warehouse door. He wore a gray suit, it was cheap but it distinguished him from the bunch. James was clean-shaven and his hair was parted to one side, like he was going to a formal dinner as opposed to coming to clean house on his rival's gang.

Leaning in to one of the burlier men who stood beside

him, James whispered softly, "Buncha' spics and niggers in here, I bet. They blend in well with the shadows, so watch yourself."

The man at his side laughed briefly before his sullen stare returned to the darkest corners of the warehouse. As the last men filed inside, the first gunshot exploded in the room. James ducked down behind a stack of pallets and made certain his own weapon was prepared as shots rang out from his own side into the corners of the room. The echoes of each shot rang thick and loud, piercing the man's ears as he watched his own group gather behind pallets or run quickly to find where Zach and his men hid.

"Zach, you fuckin' coward. Walk into the center of the room where we can chat this out!" James shouted, followed by a hearty laugh.

One of his men passed to his side and popped up from behind one of the pallet stacks to fire three shots into a shadow crossing the room. With each flash of the blast, the other man was illuminated and his fall played out like a strobe-lit dance floor. When the light was extinguished, a shadow lay writhing on the cold concrete.

"Good shot, Brian," James said with a smile.

"No problem, Boss," Brian returned. "Get over behind those crates over there, I think they might be coming around this wall here."

"Not after that bastard went down," James replied, but listened to his man's advice and sprinted cautiously to a couple crates that were set nearly in the center of the vast room.

"Listen, lil' man; you gotta' try and figure your way out of this mess," Malcolm said in a hushed voice to the youth at his side. Jason was stubborn, though, and refused to move from his position. Either that or he was frozen with fear. "Why you came here, I'll never know. I'll be surprised if halfa' us get outta' this shit. There's a door in the back where you can leave, see it?"

"I'm not leaving."

"Do you see the damn door or not, kid?" Malcolm asked, nearly raising his voice above a whisper.

"I see it," Jason replied.

Malcolm turned his attention back to the front of the room. His best friend Danny had been shot trying to make a break for the front door, and he moved in slight echoes of life on the concrete floor of the warehouse. *You dumb bastard, why'd you have to run?* Tears welled up in Malcolm's amber eyes, but he fought them back and popped up from behind his crate to fire three .44 caliber rounds into a stack of pallets. The smoke from the barrel drifted lightly to the ceiling, and the sounds of a couple grunts gave Malcolm the slight pleasure that he must have hit a target or two. Blue and red lights began streaming across the ceiling then, beginning a ceaseless dance with one another as Malcolm's heart climbed into his throat.

"It's the cops!" someone shouted on James' side.

James glanced from the door back to Brian, slumped against the stack of pallets he thought would protect him. He scowled and swiveled back to where the shots came from in anticipation.

Brian attempted to stop the ebbing flow of blood from his side. He grunted and dropped his pistol to the floor, using his free fingers to plug up the wound and cease his life from ending. *Fuck, fuck, fuck,* he thought as water formed in his eyes. *My eyes are glazing. Fuck, my eyes are glazing!* He wanted to shout. He wanted to scream. He wanted to cry.

*

"Unit responding," Officer Lawrence informed the dispatcher.

"What'd they say?" Officer Matthews asked. "Shots fired, already?"

Lawrence glanced at his partner in the driver's seat. "So that note in Todd's house was right. This warehouse is where it's all going down."

They took a turn down a dark alley and increased speed. A dozen cars were parked around a seemingly abandoned warehouse, two of them squad cars with their red and blue lights flickering. Policemen were already filing inside. *Bad decision,* Lawrence thought. According to the notes there were going to be a whole slew of men on this James character's side alone. If they hoped everyone would drop their weapons once the police arrived they were dead wrong.

"You think this kid involved with those murders is here?" Matthews asked.

The tires screeched to a halt and they both promptly exited the vehicle. Lawrence pulled the 12-gauge from the center of the vehicle. He chambered a round. "That would be the logical conclusion. Remember, the people at the first two scenes said they saw two young kids. One short cokehead-lookin' teen and the other one was tall and gangly. Clearly that was the dead one. Max."

"Dark hair and dark eyes on the other?" Matthews asked as they approached the entrance.

Lawrence nodded and kicked in the door.

"Police!" came the shout from the doorway for a second time.

"Shit..." Gino muttered. "Travis, run on the left side and I'll cover you. Then, when you get there, you cover me as I catch up."

His friend looked troubled, running his hands through his dark hair and sighing involuntarily, as more gunshots erupted through the warehouse. The door remained open, ushering in a whole new pair of uniformed men. Gino popped up for a moment and released five shots from his handgun at the newcomers. They ducked away behind some crates.

"Jesus Christ," Travis said, fear evident in his dark eyes. "How can you do that shit? Those cops might have families, for God's sake."

"It's about the moment, Travis," Gino explained as he dropped the empty magazine into his hand. Replacing the spent bullets with fresh ones, he looked at his disgruntled friend once more. "I missed anyway. But those jakes can't stay alive if we're gonna' get outta' this. At this moment, those cops' families think they might be coming home for dessert. I'll let my conscience worry about this shit tomorrow, when those families realize what was happening during dinner."

"You're a cold fuck, you know that?"

"We're in a whole new mess now, Travis. If you want to pick your gun up and help, that would be great."

"José," Zach said softly. He knelt over his driver's lifeless body. He slapped the Mexican man lightly, attempting to revive him. Gunfire shattered the warehouse's darkness around them. A shadow moved to stand next to him and Zach wrung his hands with grief. He looked up at the dark man. "Travis?"

"Afraid not," James' voice replied. A shot followed the voice and Zach clutched at his chest to find that it pierced his sternum, just to the left of its center. He gasped for air as he slumped down against the pallet stack behind him. James chuckled wryly. He leveled the gun again but swiveled when he heard the police screaming into their radios for backup. "Mother fuckers!" he screamed and sent four rounds into the slinking shadows. Two men dropped, one with his hand on his throat, while the other lay completely lifeless from the round that punctured his frontal lobe to explode out of his cranium.

Zach leveled his handgun at his enemy's back and fired every round left in the magazine. Seven shots exploded from the chamber. Five of them struck home, throwing James to the cold floor in agony. He wrapped his hand around himself to feel for the wounds, hollering about the pain he was in. Zach smiled even as his vision clouded over.

Travis weaved through the crates on the left side of the warehouse, sprinting past dead police officers and James' cronies, until he came to the black corner. When he ducked into the safety of the warehouse's darkest shadows, he lifted his pistol and opened fire on two of James' minions. Brain and blood were plastered on the wall in a gray and red vomit, the smell of it making Travis retch as he huddled in the corner.

Two police officers made their way to a pile of crates and covered one another as they anxiously chatted amongst themselves on how fucked up the situation was. Lawrence knew he would be forever changed by the events of the last week. *Maybe it's time to find a new profession,* he thought absently when he noticed a shadow in the corner. *It's nothing,* he concluded and began to move from his cover.

Travis thought about firing on them, but he could not bring himself to do it, and so, sat as silently as he could in the hopes that they would leave.

"Put your weapons down!" Officer Lawrence exclaimed to the whole warehouse. Matthews moved to his partner's side and caught something moving in Travis' direction.

The young man thought fast, brought his pistol up and mustered the courage to fire upon the two boys in blue. But their own retaliation was swift, as well. Despite the fact that he caught one in the leg, they were both wearing bulletproof vests and the second one was barely deterred by the round that smacked into his chest. Lawrence was not fazed by his partner's fall and fired back, one of the bullets ricocheting off the concrete wall to slice into Travis' arm. Another found its way into his stomach. Travis recoiled, utilizing his last bullet to smack uselessly into a crate, before he retreated back to Gino.

When he discovered his Italian friend, Travis' last hopes were shattered. Gino lay as a small corpse on the concrete flooring of the warehouse. In spite of his aggressive nature, he actually looked quite peaceful in that position. Travis knelt beside him and laid the gun down. A tear chiseled its way out of the young man's eye and fell uselessly on Gino's cheek. *My entire adult life I've wasted on sex, drugs, alcohol, and death,* Travis realized. A spasm shivered through his abdomen and he lay down on the ground beside his friend. *I could have been an artist,* he thought with another tear.

With a sad smile, Travis announced, "I should have gotten out. I should have known. I was always so good at drawing when I was a kid... I could have been an artist."

The dim oranges of the warehouse began to dip in and out, first going from dark reds to bright yellows. Travis cringed, his body clutching to life, but it was useless in those final moments. He sobbed silently next to his deceased friend, glaring with hate at the pistol lying next to his own head. "I could have been an artist."

*

"Get out of here, kid," Malcolm ordered. Despite the hole in his chest, he still looked menacing, and he stared down Jason York as if he was his own little brother that had gotten into trouble.

"I…"

"Just go," Malcolm said. "Go."

With five bullets remaining in the revolver, the first one buried deep in one of James' men, Jason stood and sprinted for the back door. No one followed him, because there was no one left to give chase. Blood soaked the concrete flooring of the warehouse, and in spite of the guilt wrenching at Jason's heart, he felt like a free man as he flew out the back door.

"Someone went out the back!" he heard from inside the warehouse.

"In pursuit."

Once Jason got on the dirt path behind the warehouse he was certain he would be fine. He gave one final look at the warehouse as the door slammed shut behind him, locking firmly into place. Jason gathered himself and began the sprint back to his brother and his apartment, not once looking back at the mess that transpired in the warehouse. *I'm coming home, Sam. Your brother is coming home.*

Jason thought of his last conversation with Samuel and cringed at the way he had yelled at his older brother. He wanted to do something. He had bought a gun the day before and meant to use it. With a few pulls of his trigger peace could settle over Phoenix's streets at least for a little bit. "Are you out of your fucking mind?" Samuel had shouted. "You're going to create peace with a gun in your hand?"

Jason had bit back, though. His rage could not be quelled by a mere argument. "You're doing nothing! You're sitting and doing nothing!" he had yelled.

Samuel shook his head and his brown eyes were filled with sorrow. "Because you slept through everything I've done! You don't know what I've done for us... What I've done for you! You don't... You don't know shit."

"Are we supposed to do nothing? Jacob is our friend!"

"Some friend," Samuel had said. "We haven't heard from him in days. He could be long gone by now. You never know how this kind of shit plays out. We do not belong there any more than we belong in a drugged-out scene. I wish we could just leave this city altogether."

"And do what? Run away? Run away like our fuckin' cousin did when some shit got heavy for him?" Jason replied bitterly. With the mention of their cousin he knew his argument was rambling and not making sense. It wasn't until now, as he ran down that Phoenix street, that he wished he had stayed with Samuel. He wished he could have seen, and all he wanted to do was go back to a life where there were no possibilities of death or prison time. Jason thought of that and felt like laughing and crying at the same time. *I can't remember a time like that,* he realized. *And, all for what? Jacob didn't even show up tonight. Sam was right.*

As he ran into the street, a shout pierced the quiet night and nearly knocked Jason to the asphalt. "Freeze!"

Jason looked at the two policemen, weapons drawn, one of them shining a flashlight directly into his face.

"That's him!" Lawrence said. "That kid fits the description

perfectly. Dark hair, brown eyed, short cokehead teenager. This is him, I know it."

"Maybe so," his partner said. "Put the gun down, kid!"

"Why else would he be here?" Lawrence replied. He stepped forward slowly, the wound in his leg ever-present. A sharp reminder of his occupational hazard. Lawrence kept the shotgun at the ready but he left his finger off the trigger. No one else had to die needlessly. "You heard him kid, put the gun down!"

Jason looked down the street to the freedom that awaited him, and back to the police directly to his left. His thumb traced the hammer of the weapon like a nervous tick. He looked at the gun in his hands, and back to the officers.

"C'mon, kid."

Jason York took a deep breath.

REFERENCES

Coleman, Lamont "Big L." "Street Struck." Lifestylez ov da
Poor & Dangerous. Columbia Records, 1995. CD.

Acknowledgements

My thanks go to my family and friends for providing a constant push and inspiration. To my Jenni, for being who you are in every way. You are truly the love of my life. To Costa, for being an incredibly inspirational young man and helping me to grow up just a little faster than those around me. To Katy, you are an amazing sister and always know how to shed some light in the darkness. To my parents, your constant love and support has guided me through my life. I could not ask for a better mother and father. To Nick and Jessi, I'm so glad our families are now fully intertwined. I can't wait to see what a great young man my godson will be. To the whole Schneider family, you guys have always been there for me and mine. And lastly, to A. Wrighton and her Little Green Eyed Press. I already had a voice, but had no idea how cluttered it was until you guys fine-tuned it.